MW01600786

ENJOY Lyk

Times Like This

by

Lyn Miller LaCoursiere

Great Books and Novels
Minnesota Authors

Cover design by Genny Kieley
& Lyn LaCoursiere

Format
by Genny Kieley

ISBN # 978-1-938990-36-6

A short Synopsis of **TIMES LIKE THIS**

Leaving Reed Conner's bed in Birch Lake, boredom has forced Lindy Lewis to make a decision. Leaving a quick note for him she takes to the road, and after stopping in Minneapolis for a new look as a blonde she is on her way to the life she had created in Hilton Head Island SC.

However, on the way she encounters kidnappers and is sexually assaulted, shot at and hospitalized, stalked and held at gunpoint. When stranger breaks into her house to kill her, Lindy longs for the safety that only Reed Conners can give her.

But will he take her back?

From the author

How can I to put into words just how it feels to finish writing a book? Sometimes I'm happy then sad, at other times I'm relieved but anxious. Although writers will attest, as many times as we edit our work we will always find something else to change, correct or add, but then finally at a point we have to throw the red pencil in the closet and yell triumphantly, "That's it!"

As you see, on this cover I have found faces for my characters Lindy and Reed, as now it will be easier to relate to them knowing what they look like. As far as their body images I can only describe them as trim and in shape.

I lived with Lindy Lewis again on Hilton Head, my favorite island for over a year as I wrote this book. And I enjoyed having her visit some of the places I delight in, as she walks the same beach for miles as I have, as she gets a dinner invitation to go on that same party boat I have been out on several times for dinner with friends. That first time was with Mario D'Agustino when he shoots a man and throws the body overboard. Shelter Cove is real and has many upscale shops and eateries where she goes to lunch and as I have enjoyed many fine gatherings. I renamed Alma's to Shirlee's Café where she owns the very famous nightclub and is the entertainer.

I started writing years ago when I learned how to identify my sadness over losing my husband and put my feelings into words and then down on paper. When I think back some thirty years when I first started writing, I realize I've put a lot of my own emotions into building my characters that are both male and female. First of all, Lindy is my main character in the Lindy Lewis Adventures, and over the following six books in the collection, we see her as a loving housewife, then a depressed woman, a scheming widow and finally a single-minded woman. In Moonbeams and Moonbeams Too I introduced Daisy Odell, an innocent woman thrown into the path of killers. In Almighty and Almighty Too I give retired Sheriff Jesse Ortega from Birch Lake another adventure. The characters seem very real to me as they have lived in my head for years. As I continue on my next book I have new characters knocking at my door demanding entrance into the real world.

Thank you, my dear readers for your lasting support and love, and I'm hoping my writing continues to keep you up late into night reading my books.

Always, Lyn

Another wonderfully written book that will take you on a ride of SUSPENSE, LAUGHTER, ROMANCE AND FUN.

---Danielle Thayer Landa

Lyn's COLORFUL AND CHARMING characters are here again to keep us entertained.

---Deloris K

I feel like I know her CHARACTERS, almost like THEY are from my hometown or part of my family.

---Karen S

Her CHARACTERS are a combination of IDEAS, ACTIONS and REACTIONS.

---THE TRF TIMES

We all live vicariously through LINDY LEWIS, an adventuresome lady for sure.

---Judy Anderson

With her charming and exciting talent, Lyn has written another BEST SELLER!

---Val T

I look forward to a glass of wine and LYN'S NEW BOOK. Is there anything better than that on a spring night?

---Victoria R Los Angeles, Ca.

Books by Lyn Miller LaCoursiere

Nightmares and Dreams

Tomorrow's Rain

Sunsets

Suddenly Summer

The Early Years

Silence

Moonbeams

Moonbeams Too

Almighty

Almighty Too

Times Like This

Acknowledgements

I wish to thank Val and Jennifer
for editing this book.
Mary M
again, for her technical help.

Also, thanks to my
Nightwriter friends for their
constant vigilance.

This book is dedicated
to
Sharon Lee,
my sister.

-1-

The woods were ablaze with their autumn colors of red, gold and orange as Lindy Lewis sped hurriedly out of Birch Lake and headed south. As she had sat at the counter at the Woodsman Café with Flo earlier that day, she had thought ahead to the time when he would show up, what then? After the bliss of their reunion, would she be content to spend an endless, long, cold winter here in his bed? She didn't think so!

They had been talking about Reed Conners, Lindy's now and again boyfriend. When Flo had asked, "Well, my girl, where is that man?"

Lindy had stumbled over her words as she mumbled her reply. "He's been on a case with an old friend and it's taking him forever to wrap it up."

She crossed her bare legs and checked to see how the light reflected off the new color on her toes. She had just come from having a pedicure.

"It seems like I haven't seen him around here for weeks," Flo remarked. The lunch crowd had left and the place was empty except for Olaf, who still sat at the counter by himself sucking his teeth after eating and calmly staring off into space after listening to their conversation.

"Seems to me, he should stay here and not run around the country like he does. What in the world does he do anyway?"

Lindy took a drink of her coffee and put her cup down. "He's an investigator Flo, remember!" She explained again.

"Well, he could investigate something around here couldn't he?"

"Nah," Olaf chimed in. "He's big time!"

Lindy had gathered her purse and hurried out to her Lexus. She had always loved the beauty of Reed's place and now as she turned into the driveway she saw that the lawn crew had been there and mowed the grass. The place was trimmed and plucked to perfection again. At one time she had thought about pitching in and doing the yard work for Reed, but then realized she didn't even know how to start a mower let alone pilot it around in circles like that. Lordy, she could cut a foot off. Lindy hurried into the house as her thoughts ran wild.

And without worrying about it any further, she gathered her money from its new hiding place behind the dresser, pulled her suitcases out of the closet and began emptying the drawers. It didn't take long to collect her make-up out of the bathroom, and within an hour she was on the road out of Birch Lake. She'd left a note for Reed thanking him for letting her stay so long but that she was leaving. And with a heavy heart said she loved him but it was just not enough! She was lonely and needed the action and excitement of a large city.

Now after being on the road for hours, darkness was nearing and she was finally heading into Minneapolis. She was dog-tired and leaving the largest suitcase in the trunk of the car, she grabbed a small one and checked into a hotel. She ordered room service and had a margarita and a steak. Then began the list of things she had to do in the morning. First was a date at a salon for the works. She had been a redhead the last few months and now she wanted a new look. Maybe go blonde again. Also get a new line of make-up. Lordy, hard as it was for her to admit it, she was a middle-aged woman of fifty-two, and those fine lines had mysteriously crept up on her. And she needed to get out of jeans and t-shirts and shop for some classy skirts and dresses. Then, she'd go to the bank and visit her money. The list done, she set the alarm on her cell phone for eight o'clock and slept soundly. The chiming bells on it woke her in the morning, and then the realization of being in a hotel after leaving Birch Lake righted itself in her thoughts.

And oh my God, she had left Reed. She checked her cell and saw again that he still hadn't returned her calls. But then she had sensed a detached manner from him lately, even before he left to help his buddy down south. A sharp pain shot through her stomach and she almost felt like crying, but she furiously wiped at a tear. Was it loneliness? Of course, it was she knew, but she'd get over it.

She showered and was lucky enough to get right into her favorite Minneapolis salon with Judy Lee, her stylist from way back.

"Hey girlfriend, where have you been?" She was greeted as Judy Lee led her to a chair and ran a hand through her hair, "My God girl, what have you done here?" And before Lindy knew it, she was stretched out backwards in the chair with her head in the sink.

"Are you going to stay here in Minneapolis now?" Judy Lee asked as she opened bottles and jars and busily foamed up her roots.

"For some time," Lindy remarked, "I haven't decided yet for how long."

"Well, I heard you were up north in Birch Lake with Reed Conners again." And Judy Lee went on, "Why don't you two just get married and settle down with each other for good?"

Lindy swallowed hard over a sudden lump in her throat and then said, "It's way too late now."

"So, you're just going to drift around on your own then?" Judy Lee said shaking her head at her friend.

Lindy took a minute. "It looks that way."

Soon Judy Lee had her shampooed and sat her up saying, "Okay, what are we doing today?"

After checking the many colorful pictures Judy Lee had tacked on the walls of her shop, Lindy said, "I want to be blonde again Judy, only this time I want it to be a platinum blonde. And I want it very short so I can just brush it with product and let it dry."

Hours later and after a manicure, Lindy emerged a stunning blonde after trying out and then purchasing Judy Lee's new line of make-up. As she looked in one of the mirrors she saw a slim, blonde, and beautifully-coiffed woman.

Now she needed some new outfits for her travels, as the D'Agustino's had shredded all her beautiful clothes awhile back, so next on her list was a shopping trip to Nordstrom's. There she met with a personal shopper who took her measurements and jotted down her preferences in colors and styles. She invited Lindy to relax in the fitting room and have some coffee, as she needed thirty minutes to put together some outfits. As Lindy waited, she wiped at her eyes and then whispered under her breath. No, nope, nada, and took three deep breaths. She was not going to let herself get heartbroken over leaving Birch Lake and Reed.

Her next stop was the Union Bank on Main. She got her safe deposit box and sat down in the small private room they furnished. She had over ten thousand dollars still in their wrappers and at TIMES LIKE THIS she wanted all her cash with her. She put it in her purse with the rest of her money and then asked to see a financial officer. He assured her that the markets were still routinely pumping out excellent returns on her investments. Her millions were increasing daily.

Cripes, she was ready to see the rest of the world again. But she wanted a day or two in the city to relax and check into that new hotel in downtown Minneapolis that she had heard about.

-2-

As Lindy spun up to the glassed front entrance of the Majestic Hotel and stopped, a uniformed valet opened her car door and helped her out and grabbed her suitcases. Another slid behind the wheel and whisked her Lexus off to a locked garage. As she walked up to the desk in the lobby to register for a room, she knew she still had it as she felt the curious glances from some customers follow her.

Lola Lang, she scribbled elegantly. From now on she was going to use one of her old aliases and produced her ID cards as she stood seemingly bored.

"Miss Lang, how long will you be staying with us?" The desk clerk asked.

"Two nights, I think." Lindy remarked and waited patiently as he busily recorded the information into their system. That done, Lindy turned and looked around, then saw another man hurrying over to her. He was tanned and slim and looked a lot like George Clooney, with an Asian air about himself and was dressed in a beautifully tailored suit of charcoal silk, a blazing white shirt and a paisley tie.

"Hello and welcome to the Majestic. My name is Louie Liu." He exclaimed with a slight accent edging into his voice as he took her hand. His silver cuff-links gleamed in the afternoon sunlight, and then she saw his beautiful dark eyes.

"Lola Lang," Lindy went on, putting an accent in hers too and hoping to cover her Midwest inflection.

"I gather this is your first visit with us?" His cologne immediately enveloped the air as he came to stand by her.

"Yes, it is and what a lovely place." She remarked.

"Thank you, we have been open six months now." As he talked, Lindy could feel his eyes go over her from head to foot and he went on, "Miss Lang, it's my pleasure to invite you to join me in our lounge for a celebratory glass of champagne!"

Lindy decided it was just what she needed, as some gloomy reflections were trying to invade her thoughts.

"Thank you, Mr. Lui that sounds wonderful," She said then, smiling. "Although, I would like to freshen up so I could meet you in an hour, if that works?"

"Absolutely, I'll look forward to it." Louie Lui returned her smile, showing perfect teeth.

Lindy turned and followed a bellboy to the elevators. In seconds it seemed they were whisked silently to the fourth floor and to room number 412. He went in ahead of her and turned on the lights, then put her suitcases on the stands. She handed him a good-sized tip and thanked him.

The room was done in soft hues of gray and white with red accents. It was lovely and restful. The view outside down to the street below revealed the busy intersection of Nicollet and 8th Street. By now colorful lights were beginning to glow in the early evening and Lindy felt so much better just being close to the excitement of it all.

She opened a suitcase and took out the clingy black knit dress and new black stilettos she had purchased. After a quick shower, she whisked her new short hair up and around, redid her make-up and slipped on her new dress.

Now she felt like a "million bucks" as she walked in to the lounge and perched on a stool, and then Louie Lui was at her side.

"Miss Lang," He said just as the bartender set two glass flutes down on the bar.

"How is your room?" He asked, then as the bartender popped the cork and poured the wine.

Lindy adjusted the skirt on her dress so it didn't show too much of her legs. "Well," she murmured, "I'll let you know tomorrow."

Handing a glass of champagne to her, Louie Lui raised his and clinked with hers and said, "Here's to a beautiful lady."

Oh Lordy, Lindy was thinking. This is great. But I wonder who this guy is?

"May I ask where you're from Miss Lang?" He went on.

Lindy ran her fingers over the stem of her glass and said, "I live in the south."

"Friends here in the Midwest then?" Louie Lui asked.

"Yes." Lindy remarked and changed the subject. "I hear a little bit of a cockney accent, Mr. Lui. You are from across the pond then?"

"Yes," he laughed, "I guess I can't hide it, I'm from London but I've been here for a few years now while this place was going up." He took a minute and went on, "And I might add my father was an American and my mother was a second-generation Japanese."

Lindy watched as he took small swallows of his champagne, while she was terribly thirsty and tried not to gulp hers as he talked.

"May I call you Lola, Miss Lang?" He said smiling then.

Lordy, Lindy's thoughts were flying a mile a minute. This man had the sexiest dark eyes. And when she looked closer she could see those long dark eyelashes that she would die for.

But nodding she said demurely "You can if I can call you Louie." And they agreed and clinked glasses again.

"Have you got plans while you are here in town?" Louie asked. He ran a hand over his trim mustache as he talked.

"Well, I really haven't had time to make any yet, but I want to see some shows and do some shopping." Lindy remarked.

"We have a lot of things going on right now in town. Although, Beyoncé and Paul McCartney have just finished their concerts, we still have a whole lineup of entertainment coming in. And if you like baseball, the Twins are playing at home, and Orchestra Hall is just a few blocks away." Louie sat sideways on his stool facing her as he talked.

"Thank you, Louie, I've always loved Minneapolis." Lindy said smiling.

"You've been here before?" He asked.

"Oh, years ago." Lindy answered. Her face sobered as she remembered her college days, meeting Reed Conners and living together, graduation, and their first jobs. Those early times rolled through her thoughts, Lordy, she could write a book.

"Did you recall something distressing?" Louie asked looking at her, "For a minute you looked sad!"

Lindy caught herself just in time before she started to blab her whole life story to a stranger. And said, "Oh no, I just remembered my incredibly busy time going to the U of M and then working." She took a slow breath and put a smile back on her face.

"Oh yes, those college days were busy but fun." Louie tipped his head and winked. "Lola, how about joining me tonight and we'll have dinner at the Oceanaire Restaurant, and then catch a set at the Dakota?"

By now, Lindy was feeling the effects of the champagne and she smiled and said, "Louie, I'd love it, what time?"

-3-

Reed Conners was on his way back to Minnesota after being in Oklahoma for weeks helping his buddy, Sheriff Jesse Ortega with a difficult case. Jesse had left his home town of Birch Lake years before and had taken another state job as a sheriff in a small settlement called Paradise. The job was quite boring until suddenly all hell had rained down on the area making the news on all the major TV channels and Reed had offered to help him with the investigation.

It had been a hideous case involving the deaths of two young college kids who were cooking meth and selling it to their classmates. They had gotten themselves shot and buried in a swamp. The resulting drama was referred to as "those heads found in the swamp" as that was all that was initially exposed after a tornado had ripped through the town and torn up the area.

Joe McGreger, another buddy from the FBI joined them and the three men worked together again as they had before on the D'Agustino case. But now the case was closed and as Reed Conners neared Minneapolis in his Corvette he was tired, hungry and needing a day or two to rest before getting on the last leg of the five-hour journey home to Birch Lake.

A huge road sign along the way advertised the newly opened Majestic Hotel. He remembered meeting Louie Lui, a millionaire Londoner, who was building another one of his famous hotels right here in downtown Minneapolis. Now would be a good time to check it out. Reed cruised up to the elegant front entrance and a valet was right there to open the car door for him and take out his bags, while another whisked the Corvette away to park. Needing an ice-cold beer to wash the road dust out of his throat he decided to find the bar and have a drink after checking in.

It was a welcome change to finally be out of the confines of the Corvette, not that he didn't like his vehicle, but he had been driving steady for two days and only stopping for necessities along the way. Now he could relax as he was almost back to Birch. And he could also make some much neglected phone calls he had been putting off and especially make it up to Lindy.

The bar and lounge in the hotel had mirrored walls, contemporary art, a circular bar with red stools, and high tables for four lining one wall. Soft contemporary guitar music played from the sound system and the air was dry and scented with some kind of a perfumed flowery fragrance. A blonde bartender came over.

"Good evening sir, what may I bring you?" She asked and put a napkin down on the bar in front of him.

"What's your best draft beer?" Reed asked. And while she filled a frosted glass of it, he asked, "Is Louie Lui in?"

"He was just here, but I can call him back. Who should I say you are?"

"Name's Reed Conners." Reed offered as he took his first swallow of the beer. He saw her name tag said Sharon.

Putting her cell back in her pocket, she said, "Mr. Lui will be right back."

"Thanks, how are things around the city Sharon?" Reed asked, as he grinned. "I haven't been in town for a while, what have I missed?"

"Really? Well, we've had some good home games by the Twins, it's said they're coming out of their losing streak."

"That would be great! Every year it seems they don't get going until they are late into the season." Reed commented, noting her British accent.

"You must have come along with Louie from London then," Reed said.

"I did. I worked for him over there for a few years, and I was ready to relocate." Reed did a quick once over and liked what he saw. Slim, blonde with red, red lips!

Just then, Louie Lui came in to the lounge and reached out a hand.

"Hello Reed, good to see you again!" He proclaimed as they shook.

"Same here," Reed said grinning. "I see you got all this up since we last met."

"It's been over a bloody year since then." He nodded to Sharon, "Would you get me a beer too, please?" He sat down on the empty stool next to Reed.

"It turned out beautiful Louie." Reed said. And judging from Louie's suit and accessories Reed was glad he had slipped on a good looking beige leather jacket earlier.

"Thanks, it's been running pretty smoothly now. The first six months or so can be hard on the nerves but I've got good people working with me." Louie raised his glass of beer and drank. "So, you were in the south working with Jesse Ortega on a case?" Louie went on, "I met the "bloke" way back one time at some function when I was here."

"He's a friend from Birch Lake, Louie. He was our sheriff for years, hard worker and totally trustworthy."

"I remember he said he had pulled up stakes. I offered him a job, but he declined."

Reed drank his beer. It felt good to be back in the north "on his home turf."

"Jesse spent some time rambling around the south, then settled for a job in a small town. It wasn't much until a horror exploded on the scene," Reed went on to say.

"You must be talking about those human heads found in a swamp!" Louie exclaimed.

"That's the one! Then you must have heard that we found Angus, the murderer of the two college kids. And then that he got himself killed!

"I stayed with it 'til the end." Louie said. "Good job, you guys!"

Sharon came over. "Mr. Conners," she said, "May I bring you some appetizers to munch on?"

Reed gazed over longingly at a table spread with heated platters of shrimp, chicken wings and numerous covered dishes that he could only imagine held delicious surprises. But he didn't need any.

"No thank you Sharon, I need to take off a few pounds."

Standing up, Louie took a last swallow of his beer. "Will you be staying with us for a day or two?" He asked.

To which Reed replied. "I am."

"Wonderful," Louie replied. "Sorry, I've got to leave now and take a customer on a tour of downtown, so I will see you tomorrow then?"

And a few minutes later over a second beer, Reed just happened to glance over to a mirrored wall and suddenly glimpsed the back of a gorgeous blonde on Louie's arm as they went by. And later when he took the time to catch up with his neglected cell phone messages, he also tried calling Lindy in Birch Lake but even after a half dozen calls it still just went to "voice mail."

Now where the hell had she gone? He asked himself.

-4-

It had been a few years since Lindy had been downtown in Minneapolis and now she looked around at the new storefronts and businesses. Even the decades old Grand Hotel where she started her career after graduating from college, was gone and been replaced with the exclusive Neiman Marcus department store.

Lindy and Louie were riding in a shiny black town car that had been waiting for them at the front door of the Majestic Hotel. As the driver had expertly gotten them settled and swung the vehicle into the early evening traffic, Lindy sat back and felt new excitement come over her. She had been stuck in Birch Lake, a small town, and for God's sake she wasn't ready to just exist; that was not enough anymore. After chasing this dreary thought out of her head she smiled at her elegant escort.

"Where are you from, Louie?" she asked smoothing the hem of her black knit dress over her knees.

"I'm from London actually, but I've been coming here quite often." Louie commented and went on, "I think Minneapolis, is a great city. And much more friendly than my stoic colleagues are over there."

"Really?" Lindy ran a hand through her new blonde tresses and satisfied it still looked good, asked, "What is your position at the Majestic? In my career days, I worked at a hotel for years."

Louie grinned, "I own the place Lola," he said, enjoying her look of surprise.

Well now, this was more like it, and Lindy fumbled for a minute and then blurted out, "You mean the hotel is yours?"

"Mortgage and all Lola! I have some hotels back in London as well." Just then the car slowed and stopped at a covered walk that led into the restaurant.

The Oceanaire was known for its excellent seafood, service, wines and ambiance. She had never been there as it had opened after she had left town. The host and the servers were attired in black tuxedos and the menu was a taste-temping work of art.

"How about I order for us Lola?" Louie asked as he opened the wine menu.

"Louie, I do like surprises!" Lindy settled in and glanced around the room which was filled with classy-looking people, instead of the jeans and t-shirts clad residents who lived back in Birch.

And within minutes Arturo the sommelier, brought a silver bucket with a bottle of champagne nestled in the ice. He popped the cork and gave Louie a taste and when Louie exclaimed it was wonderful, Arturo filled their glasses and stood to the side.

"Here's to us Lola," Louie said and motioned for her to lift her glass in a toast.

"And to our evening," Lindy added.

"Yes, I must say you look lovely tonight Lola." Lindy smiled as he went on, "How has your visit to us here in the Midwest gone so far?"

"It's been good, I visited a good friend, who lives by a lovely lake, but I can sit around just so long." She was shaking her head from side to side as she talked.

"Do you have a home base somewhere?" Louie asked.

"Hmm- yes," Lindy answered, "In the south."

Louie laughed. "I've spent a few winters here in Minnesota and they get brutal at times. I think it's worse than what we have in London."

"That's why I left this part of the world. But I have friends here." Lindy said then. "And it's only a few hours away by air."

"Okay." Louie commented as a waiter brought over a covered dish. Lindy's stomach growled in hunger as he presented a platter of mussels. The aroma was delightful as she stared, then frowned at the dish as the waiter unrolled their napkins and handed them around.

Louie reached a hand over for one of the black shells and pried it open with a small fork and then popped the small morsel of goodness into his mouth. All this done in seconds.

Oh Lordy, Lindy thought, I've never eaten these before.

"Try one of these Lola," Louie exclaimed smiling at her, "They are marvelous!"

"They look wonderful," she said but reached for her glass of wine to give herself some time.

Louie reached for several more mussels and turned to her. "Lola, here just taste this!" and he popped one in her mouth. It was delicious!

"I take it you've never eaten these before then?" He asked.

She smiled and dabbed delicately at her lips with the napkin. "I love most sea foods. But I especially love it when you feed me!" She winked at him suggestively and covered a giggle.

Louie laughed then and raised his glass in a toast. "To Lola Lang, a new diamond in my life!"

Lindy blew him a kiss as he opened another shell and raised it to her lips. And the evening progressed as they playfully talked and drank their wine.

They took their time over dessert which was a lovely Baked Alaska, with a brandy to cap off the night.

When leaving, Louie held her chair as Lindy stood up and grinned. "Lordy, Louie, I'm feeling just little tipsy, so I'll need you to help me home and tuck me in." She'd had this on her mind for the last hour, but then champagne always did this to her.

Louie buttoned his sport coat as they stood up and he leaned over and brushed a crumb off her knit dress and then kissed her.

"Lola, my love," he grinned, "I promise you will have a smile on your face in your dreams tonight."

And the black town car was waiting for them again just outside the Oceanaire Restaurant.

Louie put his arm around Lindy on the drive through town back to the Majestic Hotel.

"I'll walk you up to your room and I'll call for a nightcap Lola." He whispered in her ear. Lindy smiled and nodded as the idea sounded wonderful.

There were several elevators in the Majestic Hotel and just as they got into a crowded one, a man got out and nodded, saying "good evening Louie," and just in the nick of time, Lindy turned her head away.

Oh my God, she thought, stunned. That was Reed! What was he doing here?

They zipped right up to her room and of course being who he was, Louie had a master key that fit room number 412. The two brandies were already sitting on the coffee table when they came in.

Well, Lindy was still shaky after seeing Reed right here in this hotel! She sat down on the couch and Louie joined her. They clinked their glasses of brandy and sipped for a while then he reached for her. At first, she hesitated, feeling that familiar loneliness for Reed, but then she realized she could not be that important to him anymore, since he'd been gone for weeks now without many phone calls. And here he was staying in this same hotel. How did he know Louie, Lindy wondered?

Louie kissed her then and moved down and found a breast, then the other and Lindy Lewis-Lola Lang melted in his arms.

-5-

It was the second time Reed had glimpsed the good-looking woman with Louie Lui and he just couldn't get over the resemblance to Lindy. But of course, Louie, a man in his business must know a lot of beautiful women. Even though the night was rather late Reed was on his way out to see friends.

Gina's was still in operation and the bronze statue of a naked woman still graced the entrance. The two guys who used to be valets for her were gone now and were replaced by some other men, but Gina was there in all her splendor and her diamonds sparkled on her ears.

"Hello Gina," Reed said and caught her in his arms.

"Reed Conners, I'm glad it's you," she said laughing, "I was ready to use my famous knockout punch." She stepped back and looked him over.

"Well, you still look good Reed, but where the hell have you been? It's been a few years again since you took the time to come in!"

Reed brushed his hair off his forehead. "Goddamn, I'm sorry Gina, time flies. But I promise to stay in touch now."

"Well, you better! Come on into the bar and have a drink with me and Paul." And she took his arm.

Paul the bartender greeted him and reached over to shake hands, "Been awhile since you've been in. Still drinking that Crown Royal?" He asked.

"Oh sure," I never change a great bourbon." Reed grinned and helped Gina onto a stool.

"Are you in town for a while?" she asked.

"On my way back to Birch, I've been down in Oklahoma for weeks helping a friend." He took a swallow of his drink.

"Who's down there? Do I know him or her?" Gina asked. Over the years of their friendship, he had introduced Gina to most of his friends.

"You remember Jesse, our sheriff in Birch, don't you?"

"Well, hell yes." Gina exclaimed.

"If you heard the news stories of the "heads found in the swamp", that's his town now. He's the sheriff there and I went down to help with the investigation."

"You mean when they mentioned Chief Ortega on the news, it was the same one we know?" Paul asked.

"That's the one. He retired you know and moved down there awhile back."

Just then a gorgeous woman with black hair sauntered in and went up to Reed and whispered in his ear.

"Hello handsome," Mona said and Reed stood up and they hugged. They hadn't been together for some time and they both appraised each other curiously.

Reed gave her his stool at the bar. Mona worked for the same company that occasionally hired him to investigate an alleged crime in the huge insurance enterprise. Several years before, Mona had been sick with cancer and chemo and he had been there to help her through the tough times. Now she was back to her old self and looked like a million. Her dark hair had grown back, and her curves had come back in the right places. She wore a black sheath style dress with silver jewelry, and black patent leather high heels. Her perfume was a heady brand that made a healthy man turn his head.

"Well, Conners, you finally called me," She exclaimed and grinned as she sat. "I had given up on you!" Paul surprised her and slid a frosty margarita over to her.

"Aw--, what can I say beautiful, all the while though I was dreaming of you!" Reed grinned and put an arm around her and leaned over and found her lips.

She tasted the whiskey on them and then said teasingly, "I haven't been sitting at home pining away either."

"No?" Reed laughed. "I'm heartbroken, while I've been stuck away up north by my lonesome in the woods!"

"Sure, sure, you don't fool me, my good friend. From what I heard your old bed warmer has shown up again."

Reed laughed again. "Well, what can I say, I don't turn anyone away from my door."

Gina chimed in. "Reed Conners, you're something else. But you keep coming back to this lovely woman here. Why don't you make up your mind about what you want?"

Reed savored his drink and just smiled at his friends. By this time, they knew him well and didn't pursue an answer.

Changing the subject Reed asked, "Want to go for a ride Mona in my 'Vette? We can put the top down and look at the stars."

"Maybe," Mona laughed, "but another time, okay? Now that I have all my new hair, I just had it done by Sir Richard over at Nordstrom's. I need to look good for an event tomorrow."

"What's going on?" Reed wanted to know.

"I'm going to be interviewed by the Minneapolis Tribune as one of the many breast cancer survivors." Mona looked glum for a minute.

"Well, what's wrong with that?" Reed asked.

"Nothing, but it's only been a few years for me. And you know, they say you can't be "pretty sure" until five years has gone by." She took a long drink of her margarita.

Gina chimed in, "Honey, you're doing just fine. Look at you, you're feeling good now and looking like your old self."

"Thank you, Gina," Mona said and looking at Reed went on, "Gina has been a great friend throughout this too."

"You're lucky, both of you." Reed exclaimed, "I'm sorry I've not kept up with you, Mona. But I've thought of you many times."

-6-

Lindy awakened early the next day and lay in the covers and wondered leisurely what she should do today, as she had been shopping and to the beauty salon the day before. At first, she didn't remember making love with Louie, but then the last night came flooding back to her.

Damn, she whispered to the empty room, why in the hell did I do that? I don't even know the man! Sure, I had felt like a million with my new look and thoroughly enjoyed the company of this gorgeous hotel owner, but Lordy, I don't want that kind of entanglement right now!

Annoyed with herself she tossed the covers off and stepped into the bathroom and took a cool shower.

She slipped on a new pair of red yoga pants and a matching jacket, brushed and spiked her blonde hair, and finished her makeup. And all the while, deciding to pack up and leave Minneapolis.

She called down to the desk and checked out and asked for a porter to come up and bring her luggage down to the front lobby. She left a note for Louie Lui thanking him for the lovely evening, and then asked to have her Lexus brought around.

Minutes later, as she was intent on getting out of the confines of the parking ramp, she had to stop suddenly. A man had jumped right in front of her car, and another yanked her door open and climbed in. He shoved her over and then the second one got in on the passenger side and grabbed her and held a cloth to her face. All this was done in seconds, then they spun over to a dark corner, tossed her in the trunk and drove the white Lexus out of the parking ramp. Lindy lay on the floor of the trunk with her hands and feet tied, blindfolded with a rag stuffed in her mouth.

Drugged and helpless, an hour or so went by and she was beginning to awaken.

"Christ, that was so fucking easy," she heard a man's voice say, "We kin have some fun with this one. Did you see the tits on that cunt?"

"Yeah, we'll be at my place shortly." The two men had just left an all-night bar and were both drunk and high. They hadn't known each other before last night, but now had become fast friends.

Alex Ramsey was driving the Lexus and he slapped the steering wheel yelling, "Yeah man, I've always wanted to have wheels like this!" Minutes later he drove it right into a rundown shack of a garage where he and his partner Abe got out and stretched.

By now after being tossed up and down over a rough road, Lindy was wide awake and realized she'd been kidnapped! Her throat was closing and she fought to relax and breathe. She twisted her head back and forth trying to get the damn rag out of her mouth. Then to her worst fear, felt her hands and feet were tied together as well. Had this really happened, just steps away from the Majestic Hotel? Tears slid from her eyes under the blindfold.

Suddenly the trunk lid was flung open and she felt air surround her in the small enclosure. Then the blindfold was ripped off her face and the rag pulled out of her mouth. She blinked and tried to yell for help, but only a croak came out. She got a whiff of stale whiskey and old body sweat off them. The tall one stroked a hand over her thigh. She spit at him. He laughed and said, "Come on lady, be nice!" He had red bushy hair and stained whiskers, bloodshot eyes and stubby teeth. The shorter one reminded her of an elf with his big ears and skinny legs. He had black shoulder length, greasy-looking hair and they both looked like they were in their late thirties. Their clothes were ragged and dirty.

Tears spilled over Lindy's face as she lay there defenseless. Then dammit, she got mad! She remembered a survival technique she had learned long ago when she had been in a similar situation. That time the D'Agustino's had left her to die in that dark woods up north. She gathered all her strength and screamed as loud as she could, then yelled "You assholes, you'll pay for this. Untie me!" Her voice shook as she gathered steam.

Both the men laughed at her. "Should we now pretty lady, we want you to be nice to us!"

"What do you want? Money? Well, I'm sure you got my hard earned fifty dollars out of my purse! That's all I have!" But she cringed worrying if they'd found her thousands hidden in the fake compartments of her suitcases in the back seat of her car.

Then the tall one bent over like to untie her but instead whipped a rag over her face again. This time Lindy knew what it meant and held her breath and didn't inhale, but he hit her in the face and that was it. She was out.

It was dark when Lindy awoke again. She wasn't blindfolded anymore and she was naked. Her clothes were gone, and as she felt the pain and soreness in her body she knew she had been raped. Then she smelled gasoline!

Oh Jesus! She was wide awake now with a splitting headache. She realized they planned to burn the place down with her in it! She had to get out! But how, she was tied up!

She started moving her numb hands, then her feet. They hurt like hell as the circulation began streaming back. Sweat rolled down her face as she worked to gain her freedom. Just so they don't come back she thought, dear God help me! She twisted back and forth and finally was able to spit the rag out of her mouth. She could feel the pain of her skin rubbing off as she worked on releasing her bound hands. If she could just untangle the knotted ends of the rope! Her face twisted in concentration. After what seemed like an eternity she found the end of the rope, loosened the knots and flung it off. Then sitting up she grabbed at the one knotted around her ankles and within minutes she was loose. Jumping up off the bed she saw her red yoga pants and jacket lying on the floor amongst dust and dirt, porn magazines, booze bottles and cigarette butts.

Lindy quickly slipped them on and then her sneakers. She quietly opened the door to the outside and peeked out but didn't see anyone, or see her car, so she took off running. She was out in the country with not a single house in sight. The road was gravel with only one track that was choked with weeds. She ran into the woods, but so she wouldn't get lost, followed the trees that grew alongside the road, thinking that eventually it should lead somewhere close for help. Then she heard a loud boom that shook her to her depths and instantly knew it was the shack that had exploded!

Oh God, she whispered, not daring to make any noise. That would have been me in there if I hadn't awakened in time! She kept on running and praying, not even feeling the bushes, whipping her in the face and scratching her body as she went. Finally, she came to a highway where she flagged down a SUV and thankfully, it stopped. The two women who were in it opened the window on the passenger side and stared at her.

Lindy cried out, "Can you please help me, I need the police!"

"What did you say? The police, are you hurt?" An older woman with gray hair on the passenger side asked, and then put a hand over her mouth as she looked at Lindy's disheveled appearance.

"Please, two men kidnapped me. I've been drugged and raped!" Lindy shivered and tears ran down her face now as she clung to the side of their car to stand up.

The driver was a younger woman who jumped out of the vehicle and came around to her.

"Good Lord," she said seeing the bruises on Lindy's face and opening the car door went on, "Let us help you. Get in, we're close to town and we'll get you there in five minutes!" And she helped Lindy into the back seat.

The older woman handed over a box of tissues, and asked, "Where in the world did you come from?"

"They took me to some shack back a ways." Lindy cried. "I've been hiding and running alongside this road for hours, I think."

The two women looked at each other. "That must mean they had her at that old rundown shack on the Munson place," one said to the other.

"My husband is the sheriff in town and we'll have you there in no time!" The older one said as she turned and smiled gently at Lindy, then took out her cell and called her husband. "What's your name honey?" she asked.

"Lola Lang," Lindy answered.

"Do you know the men who took you?" The sheriff's wife asked.

Lindy wiped her eyes on the Kleenex and blew out a breath to steady her nerves. "No, I was just leaving the parking ramp at the Majestic Hotel when they forced me to stop. Then they hijacked my car, drugged me and tied me up."

"You poor dear," the woman passenger exclaimed. "My husband will get them, you can be sure!"

-7-

"Reed, our boss has been trying to catch up with you. You didn't get the message?" Mona asked.

"No, not yet, but I've missed some calls." Reed laughed. "Actually, I thought that might be him trying to reach me. I'll give him a call tomorrow."

The next morning after an hour of using the machines in the exercise room at the hotel and then a shower, Reed called the insurance company and got the boss on the phone.

"Conners, where in the hell are you, I've called all over the country looking for you!" The man exclaimed loudly.

"Goddamn, I'm right here in Minneapolis now, but I've been in Oklahoma helping out a buddy down there. What's up?"

"Jesus, I've got a case that could cost me five million! I need you on it like yesterday."

The man's gravelly voice echoed in the hotel room.

"I'm on my way back to Birch. Fed Ex the file to me and I'll get on it. I'll be back there this afternoon." Reed said.

"Alright, I'll have it sent to you and you can let me know what you think. Thanks." The man hung up.

After room service, Reed got dressed and called Louie Lui to thank him for the excellent service he had received at the Majestic. Then he got the Corvette and headed north.

The country side was just in the throes of autumn now, but soon snowflakes would be on the way. Actually, Reed dreaded the cold, but at first it was kind of beautiful to see the world cleaned up with a coating of white. And for a while he would be content with his books and the fireplace. And too, now Lindy would be there with him to brighten up the place.

He tried her cell again, but she still wasn't answering. More than likely, the phone was probably in the bottom of her purse and she had forgotten to recharge it again. Just like her to go for days before remembering to plug it in. Well, he'd be there in a couple of hours.

The radio blared country as the morning flew by and then finally he was turning off on #371 in Birch and cruising down his tarred road through the woods and into his yard of birch trees and pine. The lawn service had been there so it was trimmed and all the fallen leaves had been cleaned up. He always loved this scene when coming back home.

However, when he drove into the double garage, Lindy's Lexis usually took one parking space, but today the stall was empty. Glancing at it, he surmised she had gone shopping as she didn't know he was due back today. He grabbed his luggage and the wrapped gift he had picked up for her at a jewelry store just before he'd left Minneapolis. He hurried through the side door from the garage and into the foyer. But knowing she was not home just then, he stopped in the kitchen and got the pile of mail she'd gathered on the table and a bottle of water out of the refrigerator. He went into the living room and sat down in his recliner and put his feet up, but then suddenly dozed off for several hours.

It wasn't until after eight o'clock in the evening when he began to wonder where Lindy was. Now that he was wide awake, he got up and went looking in the bedroom, and there saw the king-size bed was neatly made. Then he went into the bathroom and immediately saw her bottles and jars of make-up from the top of the vanity were missing. With a scowl on his face he went back into the bedroom and opened the door to the big closet and saw at once her things were gone. And her drawers in the dresser were empty!

"What the hell?" Reed exclaimed and his words seemed to echo in the house. He went back to his recliner and then saw it right there on the end table, the note she had meant for him to see right away. He picked it up and read it, then reread it again.

Goddamn, she was lonesome, she'd written! Sure, I was with my friends but I was working my ass off! She was here in Birch and could do anything she wanted. There are lots of people to hang around with and the big cities are just a few hours away!

Pissed, he got up and went into the kitchen and this time got a beer, then went outside to the dock and stood and looked at the water in his lake. A pair of loons quietly paddled by with two babies perched on the mom's back. And a cloud of mosquitoes buzzed by overhead.

He stood and let the peacefulness invade his tired body and felt the cool beer trickle through his wired thoughts.

Well hell! He thought of that gorgeous diamond he'd bought to surprise her with. Would that have excited her enough to stay?

-8-

Lindy perched on the edge of her seat in the SUV with the two women who had picked her up. Hours had gone by since she had lain drugged in a deep sleep in the shack in the woods.

"Where did you say you were when you got kidnapped?" the woman passenger with the gray hair, and the wife of the sheriff asked.

Lindy patiently explained again, "I was in downtown Minneapolis and just leaving the Majestic Hotel. Where are we now?" she asked puzzled not seeing any landmarks.

"We are by the Carlos Avery Park so it's mostly all woods here for miles. Anoka is the next town just down the road."

Lindy was relieved, as her thoughts were going a mile a minute. Just maybe those assholes hadn't gotten too far away yet. When they got into the town and she saw a gas station up ahead she exclaimed, "Could you please stop a minute, I need to run in and get a bottle of water."

And without question, the woman drove in and Lindy jumped out and ran in. Not stopping to buy anything, she headed right for the back door and ran out through the alley and around to the next block. She had to find her damn car first, hopefully with her money still in it before the law got involved! Or circumstances might place her under suspicion of robbery if they found her cash. By chance, her car could still be in the vicinity with her suitcases still hidden under the cover of boxes and clothes on hangers.

Just thinking of those gross men gave her the "willies" but maybe, they would have stopped for some more liquor to fuel their already sickening actions. She waved her arms frantically as a convertible came around the corner. The driver stopped.

"Are you in trouble?" a young girl with a pony tail asked leaning out. Another girl looked on.

"Could you help me please, my name is Lola and my old boyfriend just stole my car along with my purse and money. I think he might have gone to a nearby bar. Any chance you could take me by the bars in this town, I mean just the parking lots!"

"Sure Lola. I'm Sarah and this is my sister Pier. There's only a few bars here in Anoka!"

"Thank you, thank you," Lindy whispered. "It's a white Lexus with the plates LML 7936." They didn't need to hear the real story, and Lindy climbed in as the driver stepped on the gas.

Lindy felt for the zippered pocket of her yoga pants where the two fifty-dollar bills, she always kept there for emergencies, were still safe. Thankfully they were still there.

"Okay, lady here we are," Sarah, the driver exclaimed minutes later. The neon lights from a bar lit up the front and the throbbing music seemed to vibrate through the ground and up into the vehicle.

They went through the big lot of parked cars, then up and down several streets nearby. Then they went to the next two bars, but to no avail. They didn't find her Lexus. Lindy was feeling totally exhausted now after all that had happened, and seeing her tears Sarah said, "Lola, there is one more bar here in town that we can check. Maybe we'll find your car there."

"Okay," Lindy whispered and swiped at her eyes. Sarah swung the convertible through the lanes of parked vehicles at the last place. And after a few minutes, she pointed to the dirty light-colored car.

"There it is!" She exclaimed.

Lindy sat up. "Wait," she said and climbed out, then sucked in her breath as she recognized her car and saw her lipstick and sunglasses inside on the arm rest! It was dirty, but stepping closer and peering into the back seat, she saw that the boxes and hangers of clothes she had covered the suitcases with were still there. Beer cans and fast food cartons had been tossed in, but she could see a corner of one of her suitcases! She went over and reached under the front fender and retrieved her hidden extra set of keys.

"Follow me," She exclaimed to the girls in the convertible and jumped in and thank God, her Lexis started! She'd taken back her own car and couldn't get away from there fast enough. A few blocks further on, she pulled over and the girls in the convertible followed.

"Thank you for helping me," she said and handed them each a fifty-dollar bill.

"We were glad to do it. Are you going to be okay now though?" Pier asked.

Lindy assured them she was fine and thanked the girls again for their help. She drove on then for some time still too shell-shocked to make a plan of action, but she soon found herself on the freeway leading south away from Minneapolis. No way was she going to report this sexual assault and theft to the sheriff and have to go to an emergency hospital and get into their system. She was taking birth control pills faithfully so no danger there, but she would have to find a clinic soon and get a HIV test done just to make sure she hadn't been exposed. For now, she had to find a place to take a shower and get the stink of those men off her body. So, she continued driving and would stop at the first motel she came to for the night.

As she drove however, she realized she could have gone back to Birch Lake and let Reed take care of her, but instinct had led her away. So, she drove on.

And thinking back over the last couple days reminded her of the pitfalls of traveling alone. Especially how easy it had been the day before for those men to grab her and disappear to that hideout in the woods. She shivered just thinking about them. As much as she hated to, she had to admit, it was beneficial she had been out of it when they had done their ravishing or she could have been dead by now!

-9-

Sitting there in his recliner, it felt good to Reed to be home after being down south in Oklahoma. And he was relieved for his friend Jesse that the case of the missing bodies had been solved and the murder book closed. Now, the Federated Insurance Company that he did investigative work for had a claim for five million and needed him to check it out. "Something about this is fishy!" His boss had exclaimed. It had been a car accident where their insured driver had hit a senior citizen.

Goddamn, he growled to the walls, I was looking forward to enjoying a peaceful fall with Lindy here to appreciate it with me. Now, she's gone! And now I'll have to leave again too! The sudden irritation of it all gave him enough energy to attack the piled-up mail and he spent time paying the bills, then threw the rest of the junk in the garbage and finally went to bed. His sleep was a jumble of headless bodies, Lindy in tears and the hot sweaty south.

He awoke at daybreak and without taking time even for coffee, he went down to the dock and climbed into his boat. It had been weeks since he had been on the water and now he took some time to just enjoy the beautiful fall colors of the surrounding trees. Today the sky was a brilliant blue and he watched an eagle as it soared lazily back and forth on the air currents. It was pure heaven!

After a shower and breakfast, he settled in his office with his second cup of coffee. The file from the Federated Insurance Company had been delivered to his door earlier.

Jason Edwards lived in Billings, Montana and was insured by Federated. He was being sued by Inga Mueller for five million dollars. She was seventy-nine years old and charged that she was making a left turn when he came out of nowhere and hit her. She was driving an older Buick and he had a silver pickup. She was not physically hurt but mentally she needed specialized care.

Reed read the file through once. He always liked to put the report aside for a few hours and let the file soak in. So, he drove into Birch and within a few minutes he was already settling on a stool at the

Woodsmen Café with his old friends who were lined up in various stages of eating their lunch/dinner.

"Hey buddy," he said to Ed Harrison, who owned the auto dealership in town and who was known for miles around.

"Reed Conners, how the hell are you?' Ed asked and grinned.

"Great and glad to be back." Reed said and ordered a burger from Flo, an octogenarian and waitress. "Last I heard you and Daisy O'Dell had flown the coop!" He remarked to Ed.

"That's true," Ed exclaimed. "We had a good time, and she stayed with me for a few weeks when we got back, but then, she left to settle some things, she said."

Then not seeing any crutches. "The legs okay now?" Reed asked his good friend. Ed had been shot in both knees several years ago by a killer who was out to get Daisy O'Dell.

Ed nodded, "Almost good as new." Then went on, "Actually I don't know about Daisy, but like they say, I guess we're "friends with benefits!"

Stan the owner of the café had come and joined the group. He was a single man too.

"Sounds like the way to go though." he grinned. "Don't get tangled up with women, I learned my lesson years ago. You'll just get burned in the end!"

The consensus was then of agreement and the guys scowled and shook their heads. Flo came by with the coffee pot and refilled their cups but remarked, seeing the sudden gloomy faces of her customers at the counter.

"What happened here guys, is the world coming to an end?" She patted her French twist hair-do as she stood there then added, "If it is I better let Otto know!" Otto was the other octogenarian in Birch and he was already over at the Legion bar on his usual stool.

"No Flo. We're just talking. But can you bring everyone a piece of that good-looking apple pie and maybe put a dab of ice cream on it too please. You can put it on my tab." Reed said to her.

"Oh my," Flo said hurrying away to get the pie ready for everyone.

"Thanks Reed," the guys said, "It might be just what we need for now, until it's a respectable time to join Otto next door." Now they all smiled and waited expectantly for their dessert.

"So, you're going to Montana to do some investigating then?" Ed asked.

"Yeah I'm going to Billings. I've never been there so this should be interesting." Reed ran a hand through his hair.

"I got up around that area once on a hunting trip," Stan remarked. "Ah-- that was the beginning of my marriage going to hell." He shook his head and blew out a breath. "Be careful Reed, up around those cowgirls!"

"Yup, thanks Stan," Reed commented and then they watched as Flo brought over a large tray of the apple pie with scoops of vanilla ice cream toppling over each piece.

Reed went on as they all licked their lips in appreciation of the goodies. "Ed, I've got to have my 'Vette looked over today so okay if I bring it by your service center for a tune-up?"

"Hell, follow me back there now and drop it off and I'll drive you home. But it'll cost you a beer though." And then it was quiet as the guys dived into their hot cinnamon apple pie and ice cream.

Later back home Reed began to make the arrangements for his trip. He found a five-star hotel in downtown Billings that looked good. It had all the amenities like a restaurant/bar, a workout room, and indoor and outdoor pool. He reserved it for a week for now and would reschedule later when he had a better idea of how long this investigation would take. He gathered his clothes and called his neighbor again to keep an eye on his place.

The next morning, he got on the road with the hope he could finish this job in a few days and be back home. He liked to get going early in the morning, so today after several cups of coffee and a shower, Reed was ready.

The sun was burning off the frost in the ditches as he drove over and around the hills through Nisswa. The roads were not busy as most of the tourists were gone this time of year and most of the residents were still enjoying their breakfast. Reed put a Willie Nelson CD on and settled back with a cigarette as he drove.

Billings was the largest city in the state of Montana, and the colorful advertising signs along the way were a welcome change from the miles and miles of nothingness. The speed limit was 85 miles an hour, and when clear, he punched the Corvette close to ninety.

He had driven with stops only for food, gas and restroom breaks along the way as he wanted to get to his destination and then sleep. Being on the road for over fourteen hours now but with the end in sight, he had to summon up his last dregs of energy.

He had reservations at the Northern Hotel, a fairly new establishment. As Reed drove up under a covered portico he grabbed his luggage, and a valet parked his car in a covered garage. The hotel was located in the heart of downtown Billings.

The lobby in the Northern Hotel was upscale but he was too fagged out to appreciate the opulent design and within a few minutes he was installed in his room and in bed. Sleep came almost right away.

Early the next morning after room service and then a pot of coffee, Reed took out the file again and reread it. First of all, he needed to meet Edwards so he looked up the man's address and the GPS led him to the outskirts of town.

Jason Edwards' home had been a farm or a ranch in its day, but now the buildings stood old and forlorn in need of paint and repair. A barn stood with a bowed roof and the upstairs hayloft doorway was open with tufts of hay spilling out. Barn swallows flew about and squawked at the interference as Reed drove in. Several other smaller buildings stood in the yard amidst rusty machinery left here and there with tall grass and weeds claiming their own room amongst the aging place. Reed parked in a turn around by the barn and walked to the house. He went up a high porch of wooden steps and knocked, then again.

"Jesus Christ, hold your horses." A man's voice echoed. "I'll be there as soon as I can." And then Reed could hear footsteps and after a good five minutes the door creaked open and the gruff voice appeared to have come from a youngish-looking man.

"Who the hell are you and what do you want?" He growled.

Reed had his ID ready. "Name's Reed Conners, are you Jason Edwards?"

"You found me," The man said.

"Mr. Edwards, I'm here from Federated, your insurance company, and as you are the defendant in a claim I'm here to look into it for you."

Edwards looked at Reed, and muttered under his breath, "Hell, now what?"

-10-

The crowd was clapping to the music and working up to a frenzy as CeCe slipped off her clothes and quickly into the rhinestone spangled G-string and pasties. She bent over at the waist and swished her long hair around and when she straightened up it fell down into a tangled mass of blonde curls. Slipping into her high heels she hit the stage just in time to the crescendo as Clark, the emcee exclaimed, "Here she is, the sexy, the beautiful, the woman of your dreams, Miss CeCe Jones!" And as the spotlight fell on her, she was already making love to the pole. This always set the pace as the mostly male audience got to their feet and cheered and clapped. And the expertly trained cocktail waitresses hustled through the crowd and doubled their orders as the guys thirst buds were exhilarated by the tempo of the night.

Headliner, Alicia Mueller or CeCe Jones as she was called, did her routine automatically tonight as she had been on the circuit for years now and it came easy for her to smile at the gawking men and watch them toss their money to her. When it looked like they were not paying strict attention, she whirled around the stage and did a shimmy almost right in their faces. This always did the trick and they opened their wallets. She was only required to be on stage for twelve minutes in each of the three hour-long shows, which she shared tonight with three other girls. There was Maryann, Andrey, and Diane. Three of them traveled here to Minneapolis with Clark, their promoter, in a limo which he owned and drove, except, Maryann who lived here and joined them whenever they came to town.

"Did you see that dark-haired Adonis by the door?" She whispered as she ran back into their dressing room after her number out there.

"Oh Lord, how could I miss him," CeCe murmured. She didn't want to say anything, but when the curtain had closed after her routine and she had picked up her bills scattered on the floor, she gaped at a hundred-dollar bill, then found another. She had hurriedly slipped them away in her suitcase.

Maryann sat down and put a cigarette between her painted lips and went on, "he slipped a ten spot in my

G-string," she said laughing, and then sighed, "I'm tired, I was up all night trying to get my sweet baby to sleep. He's teething." She blew out a breath.

"Jesus, I don't know how you do it Maryann." CeCe remarked.

Maryann was like their little sister. She was a brunette with big blue eyes and a slim figure and perfect "buns". Her breasts were small and her manner shy. And the male population loved her as she flashed her smile and did her bumps and grinds. The group all looked out for Maryann as she had been a full-time dancer who traveled with them until she had gotten pregnant and needed to quit the road shows to care for her son.

Diane was on stage now doing her famed fan dance. Actually, it looked like she was naked out there, but she was wearing a flesh-colored bikini. This number always drove the onlookers wild as she waved her feathered boa around and teased the hungry crowd with a quick peek at something more, or so they thought. Clark, their promoter and emcee, owned the production and was always in the audience to keep the sexual tension going as he continually clapped and cheered.

"Maryann, can you join us when we get done here for an early breakfast before we get on the road tonight?" CeCe asked.

"Thanks girlfriend, next time." Maryann exclaimed. "Tonight, I have to get right home to my baby."

And the evening drew on as the four women tantalized the onlookers into a frenzy of flying bills and the last call from the bartenders, as all four hit the stage for their last number. As usual, some of the guys stayed around waiting for a chance to get close to their money. But unbeknownst to them, Clark gave the girls ten minutes to pack up and then they were out a side door into the limo and gone in minutes. And Clark would always drive Maryann home first to see that she got there safely.

"Goodbye and thanks," she said as she grabbed up her suitcase of spangled outfits, "I'll see you all next time."

Their next stop was in Brainerd, Minnesota a big busy vacation area of lakes and summer homes that was still crowded into the fall season. Clark put the limo in drive and they left Billings. He had booked rooms for the girls in a modest motel in a town called Nisswa for the week. And from there they would continue on to Duluth and then into Wisconsin. They would have a day off now and then to relax, to do their laundry, see their hair stylists or do whatever.

CeCe planned this would be her last year on the road as just a few more weeks and she would be a millionaire. The next morning after a shower and sitting on her bed in her room at the motel she put in a call back home. When a man answered a sliver of apprehension slid down her back.

Who is this?" She asked, "Where is Inga?"

"Inga who?" The man asked.

Recognizing the voice of the neighbor, Alicia said, "Listen you dumb ass, put her on the phone right now or I will set the cops on you. Hear me?" She yelled into the receiver!

The receiver was banged down on a hard surface and she could hear muffled whispering in the background. She waited on the line for a good fifteen minutes for her aunt to pick up, but finally just hung up.

CeCe Jones sat there on the bed in the cheap hotel, miles away from the one person she had plans for. And goddamn, no one was going to get into her business!!

-11-

Lindy Lewis drove on after leaving the crappy motel she had crashed in the night before, after being totally exhausted from everything that had happened to her in the last few days. Thank God, she'd had enough energy to take a long hot shower in the place before falling into bed. Literally! After ten hours of rest she found she had lain down in and was still twisted up in the bath towel, and couldn't remember anything after that, except sliding the suitcases that held her thousands of dollars under the bed.

This morning after putting her luggage in the trunk of her Lexus, she found Rex, her old traveling companion pushed into a corner. She took the blanket from around the stuffed big black Labrador dog sitting up on his haunches and put him next to her in the passenger seat of the car. And doggone, he looked real! And then pulled her .38 from beneath the driver's seat and slipped it into her jacket pocket. Now she had time to recollect times past. It felt somewhat strange to be out on the road again after staying with Reed so long. Had it really been all summer?

She'd gotten used to his house on the lake and had almost begun to think of it as hers too as well. She had even changed some of the furniture around, which he had seemed to like. And what about all those cake and pie recipes she had been trying out? Lordy, she had even made a few hot-dishes!

But she'd left there and had a much-needed makeover in Minneapolis and a stay at a luxury hotel. Then gotten kidnapped!

For God's sake, maybe she should have stayed up north in Birch Lake, she'd been safe there! But the more she thought about it again, the more she realized she'd gotten too complacent with life in the small town. Even if she loved Reed Conners, and she had to admit she did, she could not adjust to his way of life. She'd had to leave! But she already missed him.

She heaved a sigh now as the heavy wooded areas of Wisconsin spun by and then the golden grain fields of Iowa came into view. She had brothers and numerous cousins in the grain business and felt a tug at her heart for all her loved ones that she hadn't taken the time to get to know. Well, maybe sometime she would.

Now she had to concentrate on the road ahead, as she was going back to her island. To Hilton Head Island in South Carolina and back to her home that had stood closed up now for months. She'd had a security company look after it for her and she called them now and gave them her arrival time and then notified her cleaning company to go in and freshen it up for her. When she'd left the island before it was because she'd found out that the D'Agustino family had summer homes there. Although Mario and Andre were dead, their cousin Rio Prada and his family were on the island continuously. She had been the informant the FBI had used to put the drug lord Mario D'Agustino behind bars for murder a few years ago, and they weren't ever going to forget that. And too, their mother the old D'Agustino matriarch was alive at eighty-five and Lindy had heard she still gave out the orders.

During the time Lindy had been in Birch, she had gone with Reed to a shooting range for hours of target practice. Now her .38 was tucked inside her jacket pocket within easy reach and she felt protected. If it had been there in the first place when those assholes had kidnapped her leaving that hotel in Minneapolis days before, she would have shot the assholes. But she had hidden the gun under the seat of her car for safe keeping as she didn't want it along in the hotel with her. Now damn it, she would not live in fear of anything, or anyone, any longer period.

Since Lindy had left Birch Lake she had begun to think of herself as Lola Lang again and liked the change to the more flamboyant personality that always came over her. For a minute, she wondered why she always lost this when she'd go back to Birch Lake! And then realized she had always slipped right back into that other persona, it's what that place always did to her. She shook her head in dismay, suddenly. Well, that old identity didn't seem to be the one she was content with anymore.

"Well, Rex my old buddy," Lindy turned saying to her traveling companion, "we're going back to where we belong! Just relax, we'll be there soon!"

After another stop at a motel for the night she was on the last leg of her journey and crossing the long International Waterways Bridge leading into South Carolina from Savannah, Georgia. The scenery was breathtaking as it reached high over the wetlands that held mussel and oyster beds. Then it leveled off on land and into Hilton Head Parkway which ran the length of the island, estimated at twelve miles long. The foliage was glorious and the transplanted palm trees a welcome change, although there was still pine trees scattered in amongst them. Spectacular flowering beds of kale and bushes of azaleas were everywhere. And the ocean air was cool and refreshing in the late afternoon of the third day, they finally arrived back at her house. Lindy sat for a moment and breathed in the salty breeze coming in off the ocean. Then setting Rex down on the floor in the Lexus, she took her suitcases out of the trunk and hurried around to the side of the house, to the glorious view of the Atlantic Ocean. She stood mesmerized at the startling blue that reached as far as the eye could see. God, how she had missed this! Then she went back around and lugging her bags opened the front door to her home!

Right away she could smell the aroma the cleaners had used to freshen the place and saw that everything shone with luster. She stepped into the foyer that had a large hanging crystal chandelier over a round table holding a huge arrangement of silk lilies and Queen Anne's lace. She put her things down and holding the .38 close to her thigh she walked in further.

The living room was next and again she loved the green and the blues of the furniture and the cream of the walls and carpet she'd had it done in. Also, the sheer drapes that lay puddled just right on the floor under the windows.

She flung open the doors into the lanai, and then slid the walls and doors that opened to the sand dunes and the beach. The furniture is these rooms were a sun-blazoned teak with green and blue plaid cushions and assorted green and blue soft chairs. The floor was tiled in beige. Lindy sank down in a chair and let out a long breath. Now this was home! Why in the world had she left all this to go north?

Sometime later, she forced herself up and went into the bedroom to unpack. But first she opened the secret compartments in the large suitcases and took out her money. Back in the kitchen, she laid out the bundles of hundreds on the counter. She counted them and found she had almost twenty thousand dollars.

Lordy, she whispered! She had a special hiding place for it, and until she could get to her bank she hid it away. She put the coffee on and as it was perking, she unpacked and then found one of her halter and shorts sets in the closet and got into her beach attire. Then she found a denim jacket with pockets and this time she was going to be safe out there with her holstered .38 right under her left arm. After sipping on the coffee for energy and gazing at the glorious view, she slipped on her sneakers, locked up her house and took to the beach and began to walk. A new surf side bar called "Miguel's" had opened on the dunes and at this time of the day it was just beginning to fill up with patrons for the cocktail hour.

Lindy walked into Miquel's and sat down at the bar. It had the usual grass roof and easily erected walls over a floor of slip-proof tiles. All easy to fold up if a storm would come that way.

"Hello good looking," the bartender a younger version of Elvis greeted her. "What's your pleasure?"

"Oh, I really can't tell you so soon Miguel," Lindy joked and smiled seeing his name tag.

"You look like a martini kind of gal." He was already tossing the gin and mix in ice.

"Sounds great!" She took out a cigarette and put it in a silver holder. An old habit she reverted to once in a while when in Hilton Head.

He leaned over easily and lit it and then remarked while shaking the drink. "You look like someone I've met. But, I don't remember where."

Feeling good back in her environment Lindy said, "Really, my name is Lola."

"Hello Lola, welcome to my place," he said putting the stemmed glass holding the martini down on the bar for her. "Now I want you to stay right here on that stool." Miguel said showing gleaming white teeth, and kissable lips.

Lindy laughed, remembering the charm of most southern men. "Why?" she asked.

"Because Lola, it looks good for advertising, to have a great looking blonde at my bar." Miguel answered and puckered up his lips and sent her an air kiss.

Lindy had to grin at the obvious flirtation she saw in his eyes. But then he was a bartender and knew that's how he made his tips.

"Are you on vacation?" he asked coming back to check on her after making the rounds of his rectangular bar.

"Oh no," Lindy answered, "I live here on the beach."

"Hmm-really? How come I've never seen you here before?" He commented.

"Well I've been gone for a few months," She remarked. She put her cigarette down on an ashtray and ran her hands through her blonde hair, fluffing it up.

"You didn't have any sunshine there?" He asked nodding at her white skin.

Lindy laughed. "Oh sure, but it was a different kind of scene. But here I am and I do tan easily." And she enjoyed the drink and then took off for a few miles run on the ocean's edge. She did see some familiar folks as she ran at a comfortable speed and nodded at them as she passed. For the most part she ran by unnoticed, but there were several who had looked back with curious interest at this new face.

Lindy turned back after reaching beach marker #48 and took her time slowing down and cooling off. When she got back to "Miguel's" he had a tall glass of ice water waiting for her.

"Lola, sit here." He motioned to an empty stool and she took it gratefully, breathing deeply to relax.

"Damn, I'm really out of shape!" Lindy remarked drinking thirstily.

"Well, outside of being pale, I'd say you're in good shape!" Miguel said and whistled under his breath with a grin. "And now I remember you!"

"You do!" Lindy's thoughts ran wild. Oh Lord, was he related to the dreaded D'Agustino's?

But he laughed then and said, "Aren't you that "fortune teller" who lives around here?"

Lindy sipped the ice-cold water, smiled and commented, "Who--?" And then said, "Thanks Miguel, I have to get back to my place but I'll see you again soon." And she hurried back over the dunes to her house.

Unlocking the door into the lanai, she walked through the rooms to the kitchen and sat at the marble top counter and began to make her lists of things to do. First off was a stop at the bank, then she needed to get some groceries. When she checked the refrigerator to see if she'd left anything in there from before, she saw only a Styrofoam food takeout box on the top shelf.

Lindy looked at it curiously, apparently the house cleaners or the security people had brought their lunch and forgot to toss it when they'd left. Opening it carefully and peeking inside, expecting to see a sandwich or fries, her breath hitched in her throat as she glimpsed a big brown spider about the size of a silver dollar inside.

Oh Lord, she cried clamping the top close, then ran outside and flung the box with its contents out into the front yard. She shuddered and hurried back inside and slammed the door.

Who the hell had left this gross brown spider in her refrigerator? And what the hell was the message?

-12-

Alicia Mueller, or CeCe Jones as she was known in the dancing circles, was soon thirty years old, married and divorced, and when she was off the road, lived with her aunt in the city of Billings, Montana. Her own parents had both been killed in an accident years ago when she was a youngster and her old maid aunt had to take her in and raise her but wasn't happy having to do it. Growing up had been lonely for Alicia as her aunt worked as a cleaning lady and was gone a lot tending to the rich, while she was home alone.

Now her aunt was too old for that hard work and was retired on a small monthly pension. However, according to the doctors Inga was slowly slipping away into the clutches of dementia. She still managed to get along on her own with the help of a neighbor who looked in on her daily. But to Alicia's chagrin, another neighbor, a man that had lived next to them for years, had lately proclaimed to love Inga and wanted them to marry. Of course, seventy-nine-year-old Inga was ecstatic to have a sixty some-year-old boyfriend and gushed over his advances

Alicia slammed down the receiver after he had again picked up and answered Inga's phone. There was no love lost between her and this neighbor as he had even had the nerve to come on to her over the years. She saw him only as a lazy sleaze and she had gotten too far along with her plan for him to interfere now and screw things up.

Months ago, Alicia had been home in Billings after a long stretch on the road with Clark and the girls. They were taking a week off to rest before they started another long road trip through the western states. One evening she had taken Inga's old Buick out to one of the town's saloons where she had drunk too much and got into an accident on her way home. She'd been totally plastered and left the car at the scene and didn't really remember much other than walking home. But the police had turned up the next morning, and since the car was her aunts' they assumed she was the driver. Alicia did not step up and tell them it had been her at the wheel. And Inga had been too mixed up that morning to do anything but say she was sorry, as Alicia stood at her side and consoled her.

Jason Edwards, the other driver had been drunk too and smashed right into Alicia as she was making a left turn. He claimed that he had the right of way and didn't see her in time to stop. And soon after the accident, a plan had begun building in Alicia's mind. She had Inga convinced she was the driver and the poor befuddled woman couldn't remember much of anything anymore, except that now her beloved Buick stood broken and forlorn.

And now Inga had found someone who listened to her every word. Well, she had overheard Alicia talking about five million dollars but couldn't remember if she had mentioned this to her man or not. A few days later her new boyfriend stood on her doorstep holding a bunch of flowers and a bottle of whiskey with a scheme of his own ticking around in his head!

-13-

Reed Conners sized up Jason Edwards, the man standing before him. He had found the address to the run-down farm on the outskirts of Billings.

"Okay, tell me about the accident," Reed asked now.

"This old crone came barreling out of nowhere and made a left turn right in front of me!" The young man said. He stood leaning against the door jamb.

"May I come in Mr. Edwards?" Reed asked. "I want to hear more about this."

"I have to go over that shit again?" Edwards snarled but jerked upright in his stance and nodded.

"Well, Mr. Edwards, I'm here in town investigating a claim Inga Mueller has brought against you. I need to know everything, including what you had to eat that day and especially what you had to drink."

"How the hell do you expect me to remember that?" Edwards asked as an old worn out recliner creaked as he sat down on it.

"Well, I expect you to take some time and remember!" Reed disliked the guy and his attitude and took a seat on a bench made out of old tires stacked under a board.

"Okay," he said grudgingly, "I had the usual things for supper and was coming home from a friend's place after watching a game." Edwards finally said,

"Who played?" Reed asked.

"The Vikings and the 49'ers." He said.

Reed said knowing his own team from MN had won. "I bet MN tromped them!"

"Oh yeah, they did." Edwards laughed and showed his badly-stained teeth.

"How many beers did you have Edwards?"

"A couple." He finally admitted.

"Maybe more?" Reed asked.

"Nah," Edward's face broke out in a sweat and Reed could see his uneasiness.

"You were charged with a DUI."

"It's a mistake, I just had two beers. And, I could see clearly and there was no on-coming traffic at the time." Edwards growled.

"Inga Mueller had been at the grocery store and was coming home," Reed commented drily. "And says you drove right into her as she was making that left turn."

"She was not in her car after the accident happened" Edwards said defiantly.

"Were you knocked unconscious or had you passed out because you were drunk?" Reed asked then, "What is the first thing you remember?"

"I saw her old car right in front of me, but I never saw her!" Edwards set the recliner further back with a bang.

"She is suing you for five million dollars because she says she was making a left turn and the way was clear and you barreled out of nowhere and hit her, causing severe damage to her emotional health."

"The fucking bitch!" Edwards exclaimed. Spit flew through the air. "I had the right of way and she turned in front of me. Seconds later her old Buick was right on top of me!"

"What kind of vehicle do you drive?" Reed asked.

"I have a pickup that's standing with a smashed-in front end."

"What else do you remember about the accident?" Reed wanted to know.

"I remember the loud crashing sound. That's it"

"Didn't you see the person in the other car?" Reed asked.

"I fucking told you. I sat there and no one got out of it!"

"How long did you sit there?" Reed was getting pissed at his attitude. "How long until someone did show up?"

"Apparently someone called it in because then the police chief and an ambulance came." Edwards got up and went in to the kitchen and came back with a beer.

"Did you get in the ambulance and go to be checked out?"

"Fuck no. I called a buddy and he came and got me and brought me home."

"What time was this?" Reed had read that the report said it happened around 9:15 p.m.

Edwards shook his head and brushed his hair out of his face. "Around 9 or 9:30." He said.

"Okay," Reed commented standing up. "I'm going to meet Inga Mueller today and hear her story."

"Goddamn old bitch, ruined my truck!" Edwards waved a hand through the air.

Reed turned at the door and said, "I'll be getting back to you."

Back in the Corvette, he lit a cigarette as he drove back into the city and found Inga Mueller. She was suing his company, Federated Insurance, for five million dollars and he was there to see if she had a case. And of course, most importantly to save his company that money.

Inga Mueller's neighborhood was in the older part of town where the homes were small two-bedroom ramblers with an unattached garage on the side. Hers was white stucco with black trim and had the biggest red maple tree in front. It must have been around a hundred years old and seemed to cradle the whole front yard. Reed drove up and parked by a side door.

He went to a small porch knocked and waited, then knocked again and heard a quavering voice. It was now early afternoon and the sun was high in the western sky. Finally, a little old lady came to the door.

"Hello," she said, "do we have an appointment?" She brushed at crumbs that had caught in her white sweater. Only five feet two, gray permed hair, her face powdered, rouged and with bright pink lipstick on her thin lips.

"No," Reed said. "Mrs. Mueller, I thought I'd stop by and introduce myself."

"Oh my, that's nice. Who did you say you are?" And she smiled politely at him and fussed at her hair.

"May I come in?" Reed asked.

"Oh yes, please. Are you my minister?" She led the way to a small living room and sat down. "I need to hurry because I've got company coming over soon."

"I won't keep you long Mrs. Mueller. My name is Reed Conners and I'm from Federated Insurance."

The woman blinked several times. "Who?"

"It's Jason Edward's insurance company." Reed said. "The party you are suing."

Just then the phone rang in the kitchen and she jumped up and left the room. When she came back several minutes later she said, faintly, "I can't talk to you, you must go!" And she left the room again and disappeared to another part of the house.

Reed stood for a moment and waited. "Mrs. Mueller, Inga, I didn't mean to upset you." When he didn't see or hear anything else from her, he quietly let himself out and went to his car.

-14-

Lindy loved to be back on her island and after putting fresh linen on her bed, she showered and crawled in. Here on the island she slept in the buff and with a window open slightly in her bedroom the soft breeze and lapping of the ocean waves lulled her into a gentle sleep. She awoke the next day feeling refreshed and her thoughts caught up with her then.

The idea of opening up her old business of psychic readings appealed to her again, but when she thought about it now, she didn't feel any of those old mystical reflections. Granted sometimes before, she'd had to embellish just to give a client his money's worth. The cash had been wonderful as the Latin residents really believed in the spiritual guidance of a medium, and the word had spread about her abilities.

She tossed the silken sheets off and stood up and rubbed her toes in the white fox fur rug by her bed, then found a short orange terry cloth robe in the closet and made a stop in the bathroom to brush her hair and her teeth. Throwing open the doors in the lanai to let the ocean breeze in and putting coffee on to perk, she climbed onto a bar stool at the counter. Now here at last she felt at home again. She remembered the times when Reed had come down to see her, but now she'd purposely turned off her cell phone the last few days. Later on, after she had rested up she would call him and talk it out, but maybe this time they were really over. She also thought back to the affair she had had with Mario. Lordy, that had been a heated romance until he turned into a murderer! Well, now she was never going to rush into anything again and get hurt, physically or emotionally.

Lindy poured a cup of coffee and took it along out to the lanai and sat down in a soft armchair. She put a cigarette in the long silver holder and comfortably sat back and inhaled. There was something about the huge expanse of water that always fulfilled a yearning need in her soul. She wasn't really religious but she felt close to her God here on the island. And she would have conversations with him while on her walks on the beach.

After coffee and a quick shower, Lindy dressed in one of her cool island dresses, and gathered her thousands of dollars from her new hiding place. First stop today was the Bank of SC where she had her driver's license and passport that listed her as Lola Lang ready for identification. She already had a safe deposit box there that was the size of a boot box so it would easily hold the money. She kept a thousand out for her fun money.

"I would like to see the new bank president please," she said then to a pretty lady at an information desk.

The important looking woman raised an eyebrow, and said, "and whom shall I say is requesting his time?"

Lindy raised her chin and smiled. "My name is Lola Lang."

"And what, may I ask do you want to see him about?"

Lindy turned her smile up but couldn't help it, when she said, "It's personal!" Nothing like starting a little gossip in such a staid place, she thought, and then watched the woman whisper in an intercom.

"Mr. Wilson will be out shortly," she remarked and Lindy found a seat across the room to wait.

After about ten minutes Lindy did a double take as a handsome-looking man came out of an office and extended a hand in greeting.

"Miss Lang, a pleasure to meet you, I'm Adam Wilson." He was tall, tanned and trim, with perfectly styled silver hair, a roman nose, and full lips.

Lindy's knees felt like jelly. However, she was happy she was wearing her three-inch heels, the ones a friend had called her "hooker shoes." She raised her hand to his and he helped her stand.

"Come into my office," he said taking her arm and leading her down past several doors to his and then shut the door.

"Sit down Miss Lang, now what can I help you with?" Mr. Wilson was clad in a perfectly fitted black suit, gleaming white shirt and a red tie, and wore black alligator boots.

Lindy was relieved she had taken the time to do her make up carefully and style her blonde hair and was wearing one of her new dresses she had bought in Minneapolis. This one was a coral low cut A-line that came to just above her knees. "I always like to meet my banker!"

"Ah-ha," Adam Wilson replied clearing his throat. "Alright, do I pass muster?" he winked at her as he sat behind his massive desk.

"Oh yes," Lindy smiled at him saying, "I just filled up my safe deposit box and I wanted to see who will be guarding my millions." Actually, she had found it always paid to be on good terms with your banker!

"That's me, 24/7." The guy even had a dimple in his left cheek when he smiled.

Lindy checked his left hand and didn't see a ring. Well, she hadn't thought she would meet such a gorgeous heart throb right here in the bank so this was a nice surprise.

"Miss Lang, we just got through remodeling the place so if you have time, I'd like to show you around."

"I'd be delighted," Lindy remarked, hopefully sounding interested. In fact, she hadn't known about the remodeling and didn't care. She'd chosen this place to hold her money awhile back, and maybe later, move some of her investments here.

"It's been in the works for a few years." He went on and led the way through the many offices, a conference room, a coffee bar and then a small relaxing area with several couches and chairs. "This room was my idea," he said then.

"Really?" Lindy remarked. "I guess I didn't know banks had such cozy surroundings in the back."

"Well, since this is my bank sometimes I stay overnight when I'm running late here in the city," Adam Wilson said.

Really? Hmm- Lindy was thinking, I wonder what keeps him in town. But she smiled broadly and said nodding her head, "Meetings can be so tiring."

"Please sit down," he said then. "I'll have my assistant bring us some coffee."

Well, this was turning out to be a really unexpected morning, Lindy thought as he went on and asked, "And may I call you Lola?"

"Of course, but that's if I can call you Adam?" Lindy answered at ease now sitting down on a couch.

And after coffee and conversation, Lindy left with an invitation for dinner the next night with the banker. She gave him her address by the ocean.

As she walked the beach the next day, some bad times from the past came back to haunt her. She'd had some pretty scary things happen to her out here. Like when that beach bum had stalked her, caught up and threw her down and tried to assault her. How the sudden heavy fog had come in cloaking her in darkness as she struggled to find her way back to her place. And then just last week in Minneapolis being kidnapped and sexually assaulted by those crude thugs. But the ambience of the ocean always seemed to cleanse her soul, and this morning she had a spring in her step as she exercised and ran her mile. In the afternoon she had an appointment at a spa for the works; a massage, a mani-pedi, and then a shampoo and blow-out with a new look for her blonde hair.

Back home and with time to spare, Lindy couldn't help herself and googled Adam Wilson on her laptop computer. And seeing it was quite a common name several pages sped by but when she added Adam Wilson of Hilton Head SC, it immediately stopped and there he was. Dozens of pictures were posted showing him at different functions around the town. Then as Lindy looked closer the same woman stood in the background in all the pictures; a brunette and not too bad looking, however no mention was made of her.

Promptly at seven-thirty, as Lindy stood out on her veranda the next evening she saw a white limo pull up on her driveway and the driver get out and open the back door for Adam Wilson. Seeing her outside he waved.

"Are you ready for our night out?" He asked coming up the steps. She could feel his eyes go over her appreciatively. And after all the chaos and turmoil of the last days, tonight Lindy felt energized.

She smiled and said, "Adam, I haven't had a chance to catch up with the night life since being back, so I'm ready." But she had to find out who that woman was in his pictures. Was she a wife or someone special?

He went on to say, "Lola, here's what I've got planned. We have reservations for a dinner cruise out on the ocean. And we'll board the yacht dockside at Shelter Cove."

Lindy froze! Oh my God! This was exactly where her trouble started with Mario, with a damn trip out on the water. Where he had shot a man and tossed him overboard into the ocean.

She sat tongue-tied wondering how the hell to get out of this predicament as Adam busied himself pouring glasses of champagne from a small bar in the car.

She could suddenly become sick or maybe she could suffer a migraine. But as she was fumbling around in her mind for a believable excuse, he handed her a flute of the sparkling wine. She had no choice but to take it, as he raised his in a toast.

"To us for a lovely evening together," he said and casually put an arm over her shoulder.

Lindy delicately took a sip, but her thoughts were running amuck. This was too much like the last dinner boat ride out there with Mario. Could this man be another member of the large D'Agustino family wanting to avenge the deaths of his relatives? And another thought mingled among her jumbled reflections. Who was that mysterious brunette that stood close to Adam Wilson in the pictures on the internet and why was no mention made of her? She'd love to ask him that, but then she'd have to admit she'd been checking him out!

"Are you alright Lola?" Adam asked as he turned to her. "You look a little pale?"

Now was the time for Lindy to claim a migraine, anything, but she sat still unable to proclaim some malady as they drove up to a huge yacht already loading gaily dressed couples. She walked on stiff legs with Adam's hand on her arm propelling her into the vessel.

They were seated by a host at a linen-covered round table out on a large deck. Here a string quartet softly serenaded everyone as more champagne was poured by servers clad in black with big white aprons tied around their waists.

"Lola, I hope you not worried about being out on the water?"

Lindy swallowed another sip of champagne and felt some of the butterflies leave her stomach. Well, maybe this was okay. She looked at Adam and he was so handsome and so nice. He couldn't be anyone other than someone she should get to know here in Hilton Head. And after some time, Lindy could feel the big yacht began to gently move and head out to the big black ocean. As this was happening Lindy quickly glanced around at the other couples seated around the deck. Everyone was toasting each other and seemed not at all anxious that something could happen to them. Lindy sucked in a steadying breath and smiled weakly, too late to get out of this, she sipped at her champagne and tried not to gulp it, but Adam saw her discomfort.

"Lola, my dear," he said, "I can see you're not enjoying this. I am so sorry!" He leaned over and put a hand on her cheek. "We can go into the salon next door and you can lie down."

Well now, she didn't want to make a scene, and she couldn't tell him that the last time she had been out on the water in this same situation her date had murdered a man either. So, she managed a smile and raised her glass. "Honestly, sometimes I just get a little jittery when I first get out on water, but then after a few minutes, I love it. I'm okay really!"

"Well then, let me waltz you around the dance floor before dinner!" And he stood up and reached for her hand and before she knew it she was suddenly floating around the room on feet that seemed to barely touch the waxed boards.

Lordy, was she drunk or high on something? She felt strangely feathery and buoyant as she clung to his shoulder.

-15-

"Aunt Inga, listen to me, do not talk to that man!" CeCe Jones repeated again and slammed down her cell phone after her call to her aunt back home in Billings. Goddamn that woman just couldn't remember anything! How many times had that jerk neighbor stuck his fucking nose in their business? And now since he had told Inga he wanted to marry her, she was besotted. Her old maid aunt had never married, and CeCe was sure she had bragged to him that she was going to come into a big pile of money soon and that was why he wanted the marriage. He could legally take it! Goddamn it, she should just get a car and drive back there and watch the old lady and that devious asshole.

CeCe had tossed her street clothes in a corner of the room that this one-horse town called a dressing room and pulled on her G-string and stuck sticky stars over her nipples. She nodded at her friends as they all took their turns throughout the night out there for the drunks and the lonely hearts, and then it was time for her grand finale, her last number of the night. This time she was pissed and felt like tormenting the jerks and pulled her pasties off and tossed her G-string on the floor. She grabbed the stage curtain around herself and ran out, then dropped it and began to dance with her pole. The audience went wild, and then the manager climbed up on the stage and tried to cover her with his jacket. The money flew up to her as she finished her number to a hide and seek game with the boss's jacket. She didn't do this too often, because this could close the place down, but once in a while if it suited her she went the last mile. Then she tossed him back his jacket and did a fast-last shimmy stepping behind the curtain as it slid across the stage. Scooping up her money took just a few minutes then it was time for the great crescendo of crashing music and the final bow. She struggled into her G-string and stuck her pasties back on and ran out with the other girls for their final number and then it was over for the night. The three girls hurriedly tossed their things in suitcases and in ten minutes they were out a back door and into the limo heading to the next town. This time they were leaving the state of Montana and going into North Dakota for a tour of three weeks. CeCe hated to be so far away from her Aunt Inga, no telling what that lazy ass devious neighbor might talk her into doing!

-16-

Reed Conners went back out to the Corvette on the street by Inga Mueller's house. Now that was a strange encounter with the woman. He had wanted to meet her and hear her side of the case but someone on the phone had apparently told her to get rid of "anyone who came to the door!" He sat in his vehicle and looked through the file again.

He looked up startled as someone knocked on the window. A gray-haired woman stood outside the car and motioned for him to turn down the window.

"Excuse me mister, what business do you have here," she asked when he did.

"Important business," Reed answered.

"Well, we all watch out for each other here!" She nodded toward the Mueller house.

"Do you know Mrs. Mueller then?" Reed asked.

The woman looked to be around seventy, had dyed brown hair and wore her bright red lipstick outside her lip lines. "Of course, we know each other; we've both lived here for most all of our lives."

"And you are?" Reed asked.

"My name is Rose Amber." She said and straightened taller.

"Well, Miss Amber, tell me is she in good health?"

Rose Amber grinned. "Listen my good man if we wake up each morning, we are in good health!"

Reed smiled at her. "Yes of course, but did she tell you about her car accident then?"

"Her accident? No, I don't think so." Rose Amber stepped back and shook her head as if to clear it.

"Do you see her every day?" He asked.

"I used to, now it seems she's busy with a guy who lives right down the street here." After that the neighbor started mumbling to herself and seeing her puzzlement Reed politely thanked her for her time and left. Frustrated, he went back downtown to his hotel. There was something about this case that, like his boss said, "smelled fishy" and he needed to take a break and think it through.

He settled in at the bar at the hotel and ordered a Crown Royal on ice. And after the first few sips he could feel the mellow liquor start to unravel the kinks in his belly.

Well into his second one, he looked over at a woman who had taken the stool next to him as she remarked, "Hard day?" She smiled at him.

Reed had an elbow on the bar and now ran a hand though his hair as he regarded her and liked what he saw.

"Some." He remarked.

"Are you staying here too?" She asked.

"For a few days, it seems." He said and then gave her a second look. She looked to be in her forties, with long black hair tied up in a knot, amazing blue eyes and perfect white teeth.

"I'm from California," she said, "how about you?"

Reed grinned, "I'm from east of here. Are you here on business or pleasure?" He signaled the bartender and motioned for a round.

"Some of each, I have a business deal pending with a company or else I wouldn't be here in this hick town!" She finished what looked like a margarita and slid her glass over to the edge of the bar.

"Name's Conner," Reed said then and after she said Laci, they shook hands. "Have you got other plans or would you join me for dinner this evening?" Reed asked a little later and they were soon ushered into a bustling dining room with what seemed like out of town salesmen boisterous from liquor and camaraderie.

"Damn, let's eat and then find a quiet place so we can at least hear each other think." Reed said raising his voice over the melee.

"I've got a suite that's standing unused. I was supposed to be traveling with another woman but she got sick." Laci added.

So, after luscious grilled steaks from the restaurant they took their glasses and went up to her rooms. They were done in the same matching sage tones as the lobby, with a sitting room next to two bedrooms.

Laci kicked off her high heels when they came in the door and then pulled the combs out holding her hair up and it fell around her shoulders in a cloud.

"There," she said running her hand through it and shaking her head to fluff it out. "Now I can relax."

Reed had carried their drinks over to a coffee table next to a couch and sat. He put his brown alligator boot over a knee and sat back. "Mind if I smoke?" he asked.

Coming over to sit too she laughed and said, "Not if I can borrow one from you and join in!"

"I thought you said earlier that you had quit?" He commented.

"Well I did, except if I'm away from home and I'm with someone like you." Laci smiled and winked at Reed.

"So, tell me Laci from California, what are you doing here in "cowboy town?" He asked.

She took a swallow of her tequila and laughed, "I'm here to set up a show for my company. I work for a sports store called "Alive" and we have a yearly promo here in this part of the country."

"So, you're familiar with this town then?"

Laci smiled. "Not really, but this is my fourth trip here." They both sat on the couch and puffed on their cigarettes and sipped their drinks. Laci's skirt had drifted higher on her thighs as they laughed at each other's stories of their travels, and she didn't make any effort to adjust the hemline. It was going on midnight when they finished the last drinks that room service had brought and by now they were both slightly inebriated.

Laci stood up and grinned, "Well, good buddy, I've enjoyed your companionship but have to get some shut eye before the troops pull in early tomorrow."

Reed had put his empty glass down and stood up too. Stepping closer to her, he pulled her into an embrace. But she moved away quickly and said, "Whoa, thanks for the company but I'm not ready for anything further."

He dropped his arms. "Okay. Don't blame me for trying!" They laughed good-naturedly and he left her suite. But he hadn't really been in the mood for love making any way. Goddamn, he was still too gut-wrenched about Lindy's unexpected disappearance.

The next day his cell buzzed as he was eating breakfast in the coffee shop of the hotel.

"Conners, what the hell's going on, I haven't heard from you?" His boss from Federated Insurance asked in his booming voice.

Reed put his cup down and wiped his mouth. "Good morning sir, I'm trying to make heads or tails out of this one boss. There are a number of people involved and I haven't been able to really get a handle on it yet."

"Well what do you mean?"

Reed took a breath. "It's too lengthy to explain, but as soon as I can figure it out I'll let you know."

"Alright, I'll give you another few days. Now don't take too long, I've got to give them an answer!"

Reed hung up and finished his toast and grimaced. Sometimes the man really irritated him. He was going as fast as he could. After all he couldn't just barrel into town and expect all the right answers from these strangers. Especially when big money was involved!

However today he wanted to see Inga Mueller again and when he drove up to her little stucco house in the suburbs a man opened the door at his knock.

"Good morning," Reed said surprised.

"Can I help you with something?" the man asked.

"I'm here to see Inga Mueller!" Reed commented.

"She is busy right now, who are you?"

"My name is Reed Conners," Reed said. "Is Mrs. Mueller here?"

"She's not seeing anyone today, you'll have to leave." The stranger said and started to close the door, but Reed stuck his boot in the way.

"Excuse me, but I saw her in the window as I walked up. What exactly is going on here?" And then Inga Mueller walked into the room.

"Hello," she said, "And who are you?"

"Hello again Mrs. Mueller, remember me, I was here yesterday!" Reed said stepping into the room.

"Inga," the man whispered, "Remember Alicia doesn't want you to talk to anyone!" He tried to stand in front of her blocking her view of Reed.

"But this is my minister," Inga Mueller said defiantly raising her hands and stepping around him.

Reed came face to face with her then and said, "Mrs. Muller, I'm not your minister, I'm Reed Conners from Federated Insurance, and I would just like a minute of your time."

"Oh, my goodness," she replied frustrated, "But I didn't have time to change my dress or fix up." She looked around flustered.

"You look just fine Mrs. Mueller, may I come in?" he addressed her this time.

"Most certainly." She said and took Reed's arm and led him into a sitting room.

The man followed closely at her side saying, "Inga is not feeling well today, and she needs her rest."

Getting irritated with this interruption Reed asked pointedly, "Are you her guardian?"

"Oh no," he sputtered, "Inga is fine, she doesn't need one of those!"

"Well, then I want to speak with Mrs. Mueller in private please!" And Reed went over to a couch and sat. The man just shook his head but went out of the room.

"Alright, Mrs. Mueller, tell me about the night you were coming home from the store and there was an accident!" Reed asked.

She smiled for a minute then said tearfully. "Oh yes, and my nice car is ruined!"

"How did it happen?" He asked.

"That's right, Alicia explained it to me!" She said.

"But can you tell me how it happened, Mrs. Mueller?" Reed asked gently.

"Oh my, I don't remember much." She looked flustered again.

"How did you get out of the car, when it was so smashed? Reed asked then.

"Well, I opened the door of course and got out," she answered.

Reed opened a file and reread the report; the driver's front door had been jammed shut from the impact.

"Well then, did you crawl over to the passenger's door to get out?" Reed asked the flustered woman.

"My dear man," she went on. "I got out okay see I'm here all in one piece!" She jumped up from her seat on a side chair and swung her arms out.

Reed went on, "I see you didn't go with the paramedics to be checked out, why not?" Reed asked. "Didn't they insist on checking you over?"

"Oh, my goodness, I don't need to be checked over, my doctor says I'm fine!" Mrs. Mueller brushed at her dress.

"Do you live alone here Mrs. Mueller?" He asked then looking around the messy room.

"Yes, I do," she added defiantly wringing her hands suddenly.

"Are you able to cook and clean for yourself then?" He asked again kindly.

"Oh yes," she answered. Not volunteering that she had a neighbor lady who looked in on her daily.

Reed stood up and the same man hurried into the room and rushed to stand by her side.

"You have been most helpful Mrs. Mueller and thank you for your time." And Reed left shaking his head. How could Inga Mueller sue for millions if she couldn't even remember driving the car!

-17-

Lindy clung to Adam Wilson's shoulder as he waltzed her around the floor. For God's sake, I couldn't be inebriated already! I only sipped on those glasses of champagne. She dropped her arms and stopped, shaking her head.

"Sorry, I just need to sit down for a minute and get my bearings." She put a hand to her forehead and felt the sheen of moisture.

Adam Wilson stood back and looked down at her. "Lola, take some deep breaths." And he led her back to their table and held her chair again.

"I'm sorry Adam," Lindy said, "Maybe I just need to eat something," she remarked remembering that she'd not taken time to eat anything all day.

Adam waved a waiter over and asked for some crackers for her, which she crunched away on and then reached for her water glass.

"Here, let me Lola," and he stood up and came around the table and held it for her. And after a few minutes Lindy felt better and laughed.

"Okay, now I'm ready to enjoy this evening!" And she smiled at her handsome escort.

"We can go next door to the salon and skip the dinner if you'd like," Adam mentioned again.

"No, I'm fine now," Lindy went on to say." And the boat settled into a gentle sway.

"How long have you been here in Hilton Head Island?" Adam asked then.

"I live here but have been out of town for several months," Lindy volunteered.

"I have a place on the beach," Lindy said then and took a small sip of the champagne. "How about you Adam, where do you live?"

He smiled, "I have a home over on Hilton Head Plantation."

Lindy knew of the prestigious area of mansions. "Are you on one of the golf courses then too?"

"Yup, got it all!" He laughed and signaled for the waiter.

Lindy smiled too. Not disclosing the fact that to her, knowing the bankers in town was very important and it was worthy to get to know the elite around as well. She still didn't feel all that good but maybe after eating dinner she would be better. She determinedly straightened up and looked around. A moon lit up the vast expanse of water and the sky held millions of stars. It definitely was a romantic scene, and now after leaving Reed she needed the excitement of a new suitor to pump up her energy. She smiled inwardly as she knew herself so well.

Finally, she was relieved when the waiters began bringing in the plates of dinner and Adam danced her back to their table.

They sat and he spread his white napkin over his chest and lap. Lindy almost broke out laughing. Was he going to tuck it under his chin too? By now she had gotten used to his good looks and was noticing his mannerisms. Maybe he was a little too stuffy for her, and then looking closer, she saw that he was older then she had thought. Maybe even in his sixties! She was still in her early fifties and didn't want to get hooked up with some senior citizen ages older than her.

Hell, the way she felt now was that maybe she would even get herself a younger man! She envisioned a youthful male, with his everlasting mojo and blushed at what it would mean. Well! That certainly gave her something new to think about. And seeing her smile Adam commented,

"I see you must be feeling better!"

"Oh, I am," Lindy answered and picked up her fork. The menu tonight was Veal Marsala with caramel glazed sweet potatoes, butter burned spinach with Sweet Tango apples, and a Bananas Foster for dessert fired at your table. It all sounded wonderful and she was starved.

After the dinner was completed, dance music started up again and everyone was urged to go to the salon. It was announced that the evening would conclude in one hour.

"Lola would you like to dance or should we sit this one out?" Adam asked, as he led her over to railing where they stood and gazed at the skies. Then leaning closer Adam took her in his arms and brought his lips to hers.

Lindy returned the kiss and it felt right. She leaned in and raised her arms around his neck. They stood with their arms clasped around each other for a few moments. Then glancing around they saw the dance floor was full of couples, intent on each other as well. And Adam led her back for one last dance.

Unaware Adam had been slipping a pill here and there in her glass during the evening, Lindy thought to herself, "hells bells," she was feeling marvelous and when he whispered that he was taking her to his place she smiled and loved the idea.

Back at Shelter Cove, the couples hurried off the yacht and Adam signaled for a taxi. It was now going on eleven o'clock but the main streets of Hilton Head were still busy with tourists, and of course residents enjoying the warm evening.

As the taxi drove thru a gated area, Lindy glimpsed a two-story gleaming white mansion behind a tall fence of white pickets as they pulled up in a curved driveway. Adam climbed out and gave the driver a card and then helped her out.

Years ago, she would have been intimidated by all this luxury, but now she had millions of her own and her lifestyle was just as luxurious as his. They stepped into the foyer and she laid her clutch purse down on a table and fussed with her make-up as he hung up her wrap and left to turn on lights.

"Would you like a nightcap Lola," he asked coming to find her still in the foyer.

"That would be lovely Adam," she exclaimed.

"Come on in," he said and led her into a very beautifully furnished living room. The colors were stark white and black with scarlet as an accent. Huge oil paintings with that scorching red color braced the walls on all sides and matched pillows that were tossed perfectly on white couches and chairs. Black figurines topped the many tables. Lindy liked what she saw, but personally she wasn't this conservative in her own decorating.

The last thing she remembered was of him taking her in his arms and then carrying her.

Later that same night, Lindy awoke in a dimly lit room, nauseous and oblivious of the past events, and just then, something touched her cheek and she screamed!

-18-

Alicia Mueller or CeCe Jones was bone tired and God dammed fed up with life on the road. And now, added to this was the asshole neighbor who was sweet talking her aunt back home in Billings, Montana with promises of love and marriage. She had to do something fast or her plan to get those millions would backfire!

They were on the road with Clark, their promoter and limo driver, and the plan was for him to check them into a hotel where they could all have a day or two to get ready for the next engagement. Her other two dancer friends, Diane and Audrey were both asleep and Clark had a radio station blasting in the front as he drove.

Alicia was wide-awake and nervous about things back home, that the neighbor would sweet talk her daft aunt into running away and getting married now. And then, as her husband he could get his hands on the millions CeCe was planning on collecting from the insurance company. It was still too late in the night and too early in the morning yet to call home and awaken her Aunt Inga so she leaned her head back and tried to sleep.

As she drifted in and out of slumber her thoughts went back to her Aunt Inga who had taken her in so many years ago. At that time, her parents had been killed in a car accident and Alicia had been handed over to Inga, her mother's sister. The woman hadn't wanted her and Alicia was left alone most of the time in that dreary house with only a corner behind a curtain in the small living room to call her own, with a cot and cardboard boxes for her few clothes. She had grown up with very little guidance, few pleasures and many threats to not dare leave the house when her aunt was out. The minute she turned eighteen, she had quit high school and run off with a drummer from a local band in Billings that she had been sneaking out to see late at night. But after a few years of living with him they both called it quits and she had no choice but to crawl back to her aunt, penniless.

There had been a marriage to another musician for a few years, but that hadn't taken either. Once again, she had gone back to live with her aunt and for a time had just aimlessly drank too much and slept around. At nearly twenty-eight, she had met Clark and he had talked her into trying out pole dancing and it worked out. She had been a natural, and now made loads of money even after expenses. There had been a time when they had spent time together in bed but that didn't last. Now, she had a sure way to get out of the business and she couldn't let anyone screw that up for her!

Some months back when she had been driving back home to Inga's house after a night of drinking at a local bar, was when she'd had that accident. She had been taking a left turn when this pickup came barreling out of nowhere and they collided. She had the sense to know she was in the wrong by not giving that vehicle its right of way and would have been charged with careless driving and given a DUI, and she'd already had too many of them, so she panicked and ran. Then she got the idea to put the blame on her befuddled aunt. After all Alicia reasoned, who would prosecute an absentminded old woman? But after hours of planting the story in Inga's head, alas, the poor woman could only grasp the fact that her nice car was smashed.

After getting settled into rooms at a hotel in Bemidji, CeCe lay down for a few hours, and later in the afternoon she got up and called her Aunt Inga back in Billings. The land telephone rang and rang, and finally the neighbor woman who came over every day to check on Inga answered.

"Is she up yet?" CeCe asked. And then Inga picked up saying, "Alicia, you didn't come home again last night, haven't we talked about that!"

"Aunt Inga, remember I'm grown up now and I don't live there with you anymore!"

"Oh dear, I forgot again didn't I! But, where are you?" Inga Mueller asked in a forgetful quandary again about her niece.

"I'm at work. Remember I work at a bank downtown." Alicia answered never disclosing where she really was or what she did.

"But Alicia you left without my permission again?" The familiar whine was back in her voice and Alicia had to clench her teeth as she reminded her aunt again she had her own place now.

"Well, my boyfriend is coming over tonight and he said we may go on a trip!" Her Aunt Inga added suddenly with a happy ring in her voice. "And he teased me that we might get married! Isn't that something?"

Alicia's throat went dry. Oh Christ, she mumbled and tossed her cell on the bed. She had to do something. She called Clark, her promoter and told him she had an immediate family emergency and needed several days off. Then grabbed a taxi to find a car rental company and within minutes was speeding on her way to Billings Montana. It was a thirteen-hour trip and she didn't stop except for gas and several bathroom breaks where she picked up cups of coffee to stay awake over the dreary miles. Finally, in the early morning hours she arrived at the familiar house where she had lived growing up. She sucked in a breath when she saw that the neighbor's old black sedan stood in Inga's driveway taking up the whole space.

Goddamn him, she muttered. Did he already think he had the right? By now her nerves were frazzled from the long drive and worrying about the five-million-dollar lawsuit. She parked on a side street hidden in the trees and bushes.

Well, she just wouldn't let that sleazy, lazy sweet-talking bastard get close to her millions. And she fumbled in her purse for her colt .45 and waited. Just then the guy came out of the front door with a big smile on his face and without glancing around climbed in and fired up his gaseous vehicle and backed out of the driveway. As he got to the end Alicia saw his windows were down and she carefully took aim. Within seconds the bullet caught him on the side of his head and the impact caused a red mist to surround the inside of the rusty vehicle as it stopped against a bank of mailboxes.

Alicia calmly laid the gun down on the car seat and quietly shifted her rental into drive and took off. On the other side of town, she found a bar and a shot of whiskey. Shortly after, her cell phone rang and her

Aunt Inga cried tearfully, "Alicia, Alicia, you need to come home. Someone killed my boyfriend, now I can't get married!" And she went on, "Why have you been gone so long, your room stands empty!" But Alicia's room had been empty for some years now except for short visits now and then.

"Aunt Inga, what are you talking about?" Alicia asked innocently.

And the woman said in a jumbled voice, "We were going to leave tonight and go to Las Vegas and get married in that Elvis Presley place!"

"No-," Alicia said trying to sound concerned.

"Yes, now I can't get married," Inga mumbled. "And I told all my girlfriends he was taking me there for our honeymoon too!" Alicia heard a thump and then the cell went dead. When she tried calling her aunt back she got a busy signal. And after several more tries and more whiskey over the next few hours Alicia gave up.

Well, now the threat of losing the five million dollars was gone, and Alicia breathed easier. She'd wait a few hours more and then arrive out of breath to console her poor aunt!

-19-

"What's wrong Lindy," he asked dropping his hand after touching her cheek. She suddenly realized she was in a living room that was bathed in the soft glow from a table top lamp. And seeing herself half-dressed, she shrank back from Adam, as he smiled at her, breathing heavily.

Her head swam as she sat up from a couch. She didn't remember anything much beyond their kiss by the railing on the boat. Only a piece here and there, of a big house, a white fence, and of being carried. Feeling nauseous, Lindy pushed him away and standing up on shaking legs, grabbed her shirt and then a beautiful vase from the table and tossed it at his head as she ran out of the room. Slipping on her shirt, she found her purse just where she had left it in the foyer and slammed the door of his palatial home as she hurried away. She found a taxi in the next block and finally was back home at her own place on the beach.

After only a few hours of sleep, Lindy got up and put on her walking garb and took off for the beach where the breeze was brisk in the early dawn hours. The sun would be coming up soon and it always gave her pause to watch the wondrous event. But today she needed to walk and think about last night.

Why would a man who owned a bank and was apparently well-to-do, need to drug a woman for her attention? Thoughts flew through Lindy's head. Was there something about her that made him think she was an easy target? The time when those assholes back in Minneapolis had kidnapped and assaulted her still haunted her. She should have raised hell at the time and reported it to the authorities but she had only one thought and that was to get as far away as possible from that town. And after last night, Lindy realized that the banker, Adam Wilson was a dangerous man who needed to be stopped!

Back at her house with her mind made up, Lindy picked up her cell and found the number to the police station there in Hilton Head. When she asked for the chief she was directed to a woman, and Lindy asked for an appointment. Chief Sidney Joyce politely agreed to see her later that day.

Lindy showered, applied her make-up and put on one of her colorful island dresses. This one was an orange sleeveless A-line that stopped just short of her knees. When she got in her Lexus and drove away, she didn't notice a man trimming bushes on the boulevard right next to her lot, or that he dropped his shears in the back of a pickup and jumped in and followed her at a safe distance, or that when she got close to the police station he swung off into a side street and disappeared.

At the police station, Chief Joyce greeted her when she was ushered into her office and she stood up extending her hand.

"Miss Lola Lang," she said quickly appraising her. "Come in and have a seat."

"Thank you," Lindy said sitting down across from her.

"We haven't met Miss Lang, are you visiting our fair city?"

"No," Lindy smiled. "I live here, down by the water."

"How do you like us then?" She asked.

"Well, chief, I'm finding your town is full of surprises!" Lindy said as she shook her head and grimaced.

The chief of police looked to be in her fifties with short blonde hair, tanned, blue eyes and wearing a trim tan suit.

"Is that so," She remarked seeing Lindy's face. "They've not all been good?"

"No! And I would like to report one surprise that turned into a nightmare!" Lindy replied nervously sucking in her breath,

"Miss Lang, tell me what happened!"

"The nightmare's name is Adam Wilson. He's a banker here in Hilton Head." Lindy shifted in her chair and crossed her legs.

The chief shook her head. "What are you accusing Mr. Wilson of?" She wrinkled her brow.

"I went out to dinner with Adam, and he drugged me throughout the night! Much later I woke up on a couch half dressed! A lot of time had gone by and I don't remember anything about it!"

"How do you know he drugged you?" Chief Joyce asked.

"Well, I know a few glasses of wine wouldn't cause a blackout!" Lindy declared defensively.

"Explain your evening to me please, Miss Lang."

And Lindy went on to describe how the evening had felt surreal with her escalating emotions of enjoyment, and then anxiety and even fear, and then later of her head clearing and finding herself in that awkward situation and not remembering a single thing about it! "I would like to file a report of sexual assault, against Adam Wilson!"

Chief Joyce was silent for a moment. "Miss Lang," she said then shaking her head, her lips thinning, "I would think twice about this, Wilson has big connections in this town and it might be wiser for you, to just let this go!"

Lindy sat back in her chair, momentarily stunned and silent at the Chief of Police's suggestion.

"Well, I understand he's a banker here in Hilton Head, but that doesn't give him the right to assault me!" Lindy said angrily and stood up and grabbed her purse.

"Of course not, Miss Lang," Chief Joyce exclaimed standing too. "What I'm saying is; this is a small town and he has powerful friends and relatives here! Sometimes it's best to not pursue some things!"

Well, the one thing she would pursue would be to take every goddamn penny of her money out of his bank!

-20-

Who the hell was this man who jumped to Inga Mueller's defense, seemingly not wanting her to talk, Reed Conners thought earlier? The man admitted he wasn't her guardian or her husband. There was something all wrong here. And Reed couldn't put his finger on it yet!

Granted, Inga was in her late seventies, she had never even had a driving violation before. The report said she had made a left turn causing the accident to happen! Jason Edwards, the driver of the second car, had the right of way going through the intersection. But Inga Mueller insisted the coast was clear when she began that turn, and the defendant insisted the same. Now after finally talking to Inga Mueller, he could see she was definitely in a traumatized state causing her to be inexact and confused about the accident.

Leaving Inga's house, Reed located the Sheriff Department in downtown Billings and was shown in to the office.

"Mr. Conners, I'm Sheriff Harding, have a seat and tell me what you need!" The man was attired in a perfectly pressed brown and tan uniform.

Reed was wearing his blue jeans, white shirt, brown leather jacket and boots.

"Sheriff Harding," he said "I'm here in town for my company and need some information from you if possible."

"Okay, Mr. Conners. May I ask for your identification, and your company's name and your position?"

"Name's Reed Conners, I'm an investigator for the Federated Insurance Company." Reed put an ankle over a knee and sat back in his chair and went on, "I'm looking into an accident that occurred here some months ago."

Sheriff Harding was already typing away on his computer. "I'll need the names and approximate date on it?" he asked.

And after Reed gave him the information, the man was silent for a moment as the printer spewed out papers. It took the man several minutes to read the report.

"Mr. Conners, as yet we have this one listed as a "questionable" hit and run. The driver of the vehicle that made that left turn was in the wrong. She should have seen that the coast was not clear! And the driver of the second car insists the coast was clear when he went through!"

Reed asked, "Was the driver of the first car charged then?"

"Nope, listen to this, the car is registered to an Inga Mueller, but she was not at the scene when we got there. And she later declared she did not drive the car, then added, 'at least I don't think so'!"

"I met her, and I don't think the woman is mentally stable. But she has a lawsuit against the other driver for a few million from my company." Reed commented drily

"Really!" Sheriff Harding exclaimed. "Is he counter suing her?"

"Nope, he admits he'd had a few drinks that night and he doesn't want to lose his driver's license. So, he's keeping quiet, but he says when his head cleared that night minutes after the collision, there was not any sign of the driver! And Inga Mueller says she really can't remember anything, except that her "lovely car" is ruined!"

"Well, what the hell do you think is going on?" The sheriff asked. And then he called to his receptionist to "please bring in two coffees." The lady came in a few minutes later with two steaming mugs of coffee and set them on his desk.

"Thanks Missy," he said. And the two men busied themselves sipping their coffee for a few minutes.

"What's your take on this case then?" Reed asked.

"You know, I don't know what the hell to think!" Sheriff Harding said clearing his throat and running a hand through his bushy mustache. "My detectives found no identifying evidence in the woman's car so we only know who the vehicle belongs to, but not who was driving."

"No witnesses then?"

"Nada, that's a downtown throughway and we don't have cameras there as yet!" He shook his head.

"Okay, can I get the detectives' names and numbers and run it by them again? Just in case, they missed something please?" Reed asked. Within minutes he was talking to the two detectives and they just declared that the "old lady was driving, and to charge her with hit and run!" Of course, to them this was just a small case as more importantly, a murder had just occurred there in Billings and they were in a hurry on the way out to investigate it.

Reed Conners got back in his Corvette and drove through the town to the same intersection where the accident had taken place and of course, now there was nothing remarkable about the street. Then he drove out to the insured, Jason Edward's place. There, the place still looked as run down and forlorn as before.

Jason Edwards was on his way out of his house as Reed drove up.

"Hello Mr. Edwards," Reed called over as he pulled to a stop. "Have you got a minute?"

"Now what, I'm just on my way into town to get some grub," Edwards complained.

Reed knew the man was in his early thirties, but he looked like he was forty plus. However, today he was dressed in new jeans and a black leather jacket. His brown hair was trimmed. A shirt collar was open at his neck.

"Listen Jason," Reed said, "Do you understand Inga Mueller is suing you? Why the hell aren't you fighting back? You'll more than likely lose your driver's license and may get time behind bars if you don't take some action!"

"Nah, I don't give a fuck, I need to take off man," he commented and walked off to a rundown Jeep standing by the side of a barn-like looking building. He got in and started the gas guzzler and waited for Reed to take off first. Reed drove away but turned off on a side road. He watched in his rear-view mirror and saw Edwards as he left his driveway, then climbed out of his vehicle and pulled a barbed wire gate across his driveway, blocking anyone from entering his property.

Now what the hell did this guy have of anything worthwhile, to hide on his rundown place?

-21-

Lindy awoke to the constant irritating ringing of her cell phone. She sat up in her bed and huffed a sleepy "hello".

"Goddamn, it's about time you answered your phone, Lindy. Where in the hell did you go?" Reed's familiar voice echoed in her ear.

She had decided it was time they talked after dodging his many calls. It had been weeks now since she had left Birch Lake after warming his bed for months.

"Well, I'm back in my house in Hilton Head!" She declared defensively.

"I gathered that, I was going to send out the cavalry to find you if you didn't answer my calls soon. You can't just disappear into thin air you know!"

"I'm sure you've had my cell traced so you've known where I am!" Lindy commented drily.

"Well goddamn, I had to know if you were still alive and kicking!" Reed answered this time, defensibly.

"Well Reed, now you know for sure!" She could hear him inhale a drag of a cigarette and hesitate a minute as he exhaled the smoke.

"Lindy, honest to God, I didn't know you were tired of things between us!"

Lindy took a breath. "Reed," she managed to say, "I just couldn't stay any longer. My life was flying by with no change in sight with you. I had to get back to my reality here."

"Why didn't you let me know how you felt?" He asked.

"Well, you were hardly ever there so, how could I?" Lindy answered getting defensive.

"Lindy, you know what kind of work I do, you know that at times I have to go out of town to work on a case."

"Well, where are you now?" She asked then.

"Right now, I'm in Billings Montana on a case!" Reed answered.

"See, yeah well you never included me in your travels. I never knew where in the hell you were and

I needed more than just sitting and waiting for your return!" Lindy said.

"Well goddamn it, what will you find down there?" Reed asked then.

"I'm looking," Lindy clicked off and tossed the cell on the floor. She lay back down and covered up with the quilt. Some tears threatened but she wiped them away.

He will never change, she whispered to the walls of her house. Not knowing that the man had bought a diamond ring for her on his last trip out of town.

Lindy lay there for hours it seemed cloaked in her misery. Angry and lonely as she tossed and turned. Of all the crap that had happened to her since she'd left Birch Lake, this hurt more than getting kidnapped by those thugs and drugged by the banker. Did she have a sign on her back said "use me and abuse me?"

After some time of feeling sorry for herself she flung the covers off and slipped on her walking garb and went back out to the beach. Here the cleansing ocean breeze began to wash the dregs of wretchedness and gloom away.

Back home she threw open the windows and slid the movable walls of the lanai open to let in the breezes and air out her closed up house. And Lordy, it felt good!

Her cell phone rang again. Damn, I'm not going to talk to him, she said to herself, but then recognized the number.

"Hello," she said to an old friend who owned a club called Shirlee's Place out on the wharf. "Thanks for calling me back. I'm back down here at my house and am wondering when we can get together?"

"Lindy," Shirlee exclaimed, "I've missed you and am so glad you're back here in Hilton Head."

"I've missed you too my friend. What's going on here?" Lindy asked.

"Nothing much until lately but listen to this! Now we have some weirdo who has been reported stalking people!" Shirlee added.

"Really!" Lindy commented.

"All we know so far is it's a guy. So be careful, and don't carry much money. My doorman at the club says if we are confronted by this person to yell and run like hell!"

"Ah ha," murmured Lindy. And as she held the cell phone to her ear she went into the bedroom and got her .38 out of the closet. Too many things had been happening to her lately, and if she would have had it with her, maybe she could have prevented them. But then again, she might have been facing murder charges right now if she'd had it!

"Why don't you come down to the club tonight, I've remodeled since you were here and I'm anxious for you to see it." Shirlee asked then.

"Yes, I'd love to!" Lindy said. And as she talked she slipped a cartridge into the .38 and then laid it under a newspaper on the counter in her kitchen.

"But here's what the doorman also suggested Lindy, at night to take a taxi and always ask the driver to wait and watch until you've safely entered where ever you're going!" Shirlee went on.

"Okay, that's smart!" Lindy said.

"You've been gone for months my friend, what took you so long to get back?" Shirlee asked curiously. "And are you still hanging onto this same lawyer's shirt tails up there?"

"Hmm-, that's right you met him one time when he came down here to Hilton Head!" Lindy remembered.

"I did meet that good-looking hunk," Shirlee commented. "Is he the one who kept you away for so long?"

Lindy laughed a little then and it felt good. "Yeah, he's the one!" she admitted.

Later that evening, Lindy dressed in another of her island dresses, and this one was a white pencil shaped skirt with a black sleeveless top. She put on a pair of white high heeled sandals and added silver earrings. And instead of driving her Lexis she took her friend's advice and called a taxi.

Shirlee's Place was humming when she got there. The sun was going down sending long shadows over the outside deck that was full of merrymakers at tables topped with colorful umbrellas. Shirlee was at her Baby Grand piano leading her fans with the Beatles song called, "Let It Be." Lindy joined right in from a stool at the bar and when the good-looking bartender brought her the same drink she used to enjoy, she grinned and sipped the Manhattan.

Ahh- this was so good, she shouldn't have stayed up north so long, Lindy lamented. I wasted too much time there. Here I feel so alive! She was well into the effects of the drink when Shirlee finished her set and joined her. Lindy stood and enveloped her in a hug. Standing back, they smiled at each other and hugged again.

"Cripes, girlfriend you never change," Shirlee said as she took the next stool. "Did you just work on your tan and lay around on that dude's boat?"

"That's about it!" Lindy laughed. And as the two women reminisced neither one noticed a lone man sitting at the bar a stool down from them. He listened to every word they said while seemingly looking away at the ocean lapping at the sands walkway.

As Shirlee left to continue her evening's entertainment he slid up on the stool that she'd left. "I ordered you another Manhattan," he said to Lindy.

She gazed at him and commented, "Well, you'll have to drink it then, because I will buy my own if I want one!" And she got up and left him sitting there. As she quickly lost herself in the crowd, she looked back and saw him as he slipped off his stool and headed for the door, apparently thinking he'd follow her. Bastard!

Then Lindy doubled back to her same stool and sat down and ordered her own Manhattan, the .38 tucked safely in the purse on her lap.

If he dares to come back in here as if nothing happened, he's going to find it's pointed right at his private parts! Now that would tell him something!

-22-

Reed Conners watched curiously as Jason Edwards drew the barbed wire gate across his driveway then got in the Jeep and sped away. The rundown farm had apparently stood unused for years and was only a mile or two from Billings. He wondered who actually owned it. He took out his cell and called Sheriff Harding.

"That old eye-sore?" The sheriff remarked drily. "It's owned by a family by the name of Jessup, and they moved south years ago. But they keep up the taxes on it and it's quite a big piece of land."

"They rent it out then?" Reed asked.

"Hell, I don't know. I haven't had any reason to wonder about it," the sheriff replied. "Why do you ask?"

"There is a guy living there. Jason Edwards is his name." Reed mentioned.

"Well, I guess we could stop in sometime on rounds and inquire who he is." The office sounded noisy with phones ringing and people talking.

"It sounds busy over there, but I'd appreciate it if you'd let me know what you find out?" Reed asked.

"Oh sure. It won't be for a while yet, as we've got a high volume of cases right now." Sheriff Harding volunteered, "But we'll do what we can!"

"Good enough thanks." Reed drove back into Billings and by now the sun was setting. He drove around and checked out the town as he hadn't taken the time to do it yet. He had finally talked to Lindy earlier and was still reeling from her actions. And he needed a drink. He found a bar but didn't notice that it had flashing lights advertising girls, girls, and girls.

Well goddamn, he ranted to himself as he ordered a Crown Royal on the rocks, doesn't she know that I am required to report in and leave promptly when I get assigned to a case! It's not like I can pick and choose! But of course, he thought guiltily, I could have included her along in some of my trips. Should he call her back and tell her he had bought her a diamond and had thought it was time they talked about a future?

The whiskey burned all the way down and then began to chase away the knots in his belly as he sat at the bar. He'd been in town now for several days and as he had glanced around everywhere he saw the dress was Western in style. Most men wore a Stetson hat and even a lot of the women. He'd worn boots for years and had different styles and colors but always stayed conservative with a low heel, but maybe he'd try a pair with a heel just to fit in. Then his thoughts went back to the Inga Mueller/Jason Edwards case as his nerves settled. He had gathered a lot of information on the case but not enough. What bothered him was how could the befuddled Mueller woman have enough shrewdness to sue? And why didn't Edwards put up a goddamn fight against being sued!

Deep in studying the case in his mind, Reed looked up when a feminine voice across the bar asked, "Hey good looking ready for some more fun?" And a tall gorgeous brunette bartender stood in front of him smiling.

Reed straightened up and grinned. "Whoa, now things are looking up!"

She winked beautiful midnight blue eyes at him. "In case you got the wrong impression mister, I'm checking to see if you are ready for a refill?"

"Well, that too." Reed commented and reached out a hand saying, "Conners."

"Sally here," she said, "and you must be new in town!" Then turned her back and reached up to the top shelf for the Crown Royal. When she leaned over to place a fresh glass of it in front of him, Reed couldn't help himself but glance at her low neckline.

"Beautiful Sally," he said grinning.

"They are, aren't they?" she commented.

"Hmm-," was all he dared say, then gazed at the cloud of lovely chestnut hair as it cascaded over her shoulders.

Sally nonchalantly straightened up and stuck her chest out and smiled again and said laughing, "And I paid big money for these girls."

"Well, you got your money's worth then!" Reed remarked.

"Are you going to stay around for the show?" Sally asked then.

Reed looked surprised. "What show?" He asked.

"Well the panty parade!" She exclaimed.

"Well, I hadn't made any plans, but that sounds interesting."

"Alright, and you are going to be entertained, I promise." Sally said then and disappeared.

The blasting music had been country with the reigning oldies being Tammy Wynette and Loretta Lynn but now the beat changed to a drum roll. Then the voice belonging to Sally the bartender, but with an added purr echoed through the semi-darkened downtown bar.

Reed looked around the bar and saw that strangely everyone had lifted their glasses off, then was startled as a statuesque blonde came strutting down the length of it doing bumps and grinds, wearing only a sequined wispy G-string. And then thundering, loud applause as she was helped down off the bar to parade amongst the customers at tables and booths. In all, three well-endowed beautiful girls with a sway in their hips pranced their way down the bar and jiggled to the music.

Reed sat back and enjoyed the show with the rest of the males. Then he remembered he'd seen the flashing sign outside advertising girls. So, he should have realized what kind of place it was. Well, what the hell, he thought of the old euphemism, "when in Rome, do as the Romans do" so he clapped and whistled with the rest of the guys and even slipped a twenty under the G-string of a blonde. As she had hesitated when he did, he noticed she had a large birthmark on the side of her face and on her neck which her hair didn't cover. When it was over and they all took a bow, the place quieted down, and Sally returned to her job.

Reed finished his drink and winked as he stood up. "Good show Sally, I'll see you soon," he said and left. Well hell, it wasn't the kind of place he habitually went to but maybe he would stop in again.

It was going on ten o'clock in the evening and still early enough to pay a visit to Jason Edwards again.

There was something cagey and mystifying about the run-down place and the man that had Reed puzzled. It had grown dark and now as he neared the farm on the country road, he turned his car lights off and crept along as up ahead he could see the moonlight glancing off the barbed wire gate still pulled across the driveway.

Reed slowed the Corvette and found another crossing and drove in a few yards and parked. He got out and on foot went back to Jason's driveway and carefully stepped over the sharp wires and then walked quietly, next to a ditch smothered in tall weeds and young trees. As he neared the yard the old Jeep was missing from its parking spot near the barn but a small light flickered from the house.

Hell, was the guy home? Reed mumbled. He stood for a few minutes hidden in amongst a stand of oak trees and kept his eye on a front window looking for movement. Seeing none he did a double take when he heard a dog mumble a low growl which seemed to be coming from the barn only a few yards from where he stood.

He waited for a few more minutes holding his breath. For Christ's sake the guy had a dog! Now what?

When he didn't see any movement from the house after the dog barked, he figured the guy was out somewhere. He hugged the side of the barn and went around to the back and then circled around to the back of the house. Here the weeds were as high as the windows along with tall saplings growing pell-mell around the space which must have been a back-yard years ago.

Reed ducked down when he got to a window, then stood up and peeked in and saw a lace curtain on the inside to what must have been a bedroom in its day as a metal bedspring and headboard stood pushed in a corner. He quietly went to the next window and this one looked in to a kitchen. Here a chrome and red table and chair set sat in the middle of the room. Old painted cupboards in red and counter tops of black linoleum took up one wall. It must have looked handsome in its day, but now dirty junk and papers were scattered on most every surface, with boots and shoes under the table.

He stooped down and ran to the next window which had a drape pulled closed. But through a tear in a seam he could make out that this was the living room. The room was another mess with clothes and shoes strewn around. A television that looked to be a vintage model stood on a table and an old dilapidated recliner took up space against a wall.

He carefully edged his way back the way he had come, to his car. At least he had gotten an idea of how the man lived. What puzzled Reed was why he wouldn't fight a drunk driving charge and possibly spending time in jail!

-23-

Alicia Mueller, or CeCe as she was called in the panty parade, sat in a bar in downtown Billings downing a shot of pure whiskey. She had just clicked off her cell after listening to her Aunt Inga's cry that her boyfriend had just been killed, just before they were to leave for Las Vegas to get married. Her complaint being "now what would she tell her girlfriends!"

Alicia had done a lot of shrewd things in her life but never taken someone's life before, and now after her second drink she had slowed down but was still dazed at what she had done. Being a stripper, she had encountered some situations over time that had been quite dangerous like when an over-zealous customer would get out of hand, but she had never killed anyone!

She sipped slowly now on her drink and forced her exhausted thoughts to settle down and think. First of all, was there anyone else around who saw anything? It had been around six a.m. when she had driven up and the neighbor had come out Inga Mueller's house with a smile on his face, after more than likely spending the night in her bed. The whole incident had only taken about twenty seconds. It had been a dark Tuesday morning with the threat of rain in the autumn day so maybe no one was outside yet. At least in her hurried search she hadn't seen anyone around.

All of a sudden, she realized she had to return the rental car. She had used an old alias to rent it and had some fictitious papers if the need came to use them. But she didn't want to be seen again driving it. Maybe she could return it and just leave it in their lot! But not wanting to take a chance doing that she looked around the bar as another plan began to form in her mind. And after settling on a gloomy lone young man, she slid over a few stools.

"Hey buddy," she said, "how would you like to make fifty bucks?" And after seeing him brighten," She went on, "All you have to do is drive my rental back to the place here in town and leave it in their return lot. I'm toast, I've drank too much and I just can't get behind the wheel of a car!"

"Yeah?" He said brightening, "I could do that, but I need a hundred!"

"Forget it!" Alicia said. "Fifty it is!" And she turned to go.

"Okay lady. It's not stolen is it?" the young man asked.

"God no," Alicia remarked, "It's legit. I've just had it overnight that's all."

"I guess I can then," and he held out his hand for the fifty dollars.

"Listen, do not drive it any further or I will report you for stealing it! Do you understand?"

He paled, but looking at the money hungrily, nodded his head and replied. "No problem ma'am, I need the dough!"

That done, Alicia next checked her cell directory for another car rental there in Billings, ordered a vehicle and asked that they bring it to the Caribou next door. She hustled over and ordered some coffee. Barely finishing her second cup she saw a shiny Toyota pull up and a man wearing a jacket with the company's logo on his sleeve step out. Coming inside and looking around expectantly he came over to her table after seeing her wave. "Are you Alicia Mueller?" He asked.

"I am," she replied. She showed her real ID to him as he filled out the papers, and in a few minutes, she was driving the man back to the company office. Then she was on her second trip back to her old homestead.

As she pulled up to her aunt's house, a police car with two uniformed officers stopped her.

"Who are you?" They asked.

"I live here, Inga's my aunt!" Alicia said. "I need to see her!"

"Why?" The shorter of the two stepped closer and stuck his face close to hers.

"Because she called me, what the hell is happening here?" Alicia turned the car off and opened the door and climbed out making him step back.

"Wait, you can't do this. This is a crime scene!" The taller of the two said and stepped in front of her.

"Watch me! She called me to hurry over!" Alicia said and marched on and lifted the police tape over her head and avoiding the scene around the bloody vehicle, ran into the house. Her Aunt Inga was sitting on the couch in the living room with some strangers. When she saw Alicia come in she jumped up and ran into her arms. And Alicia did the expected thing and murmured assurances that things would be alright.

"He's dead Alicia!" She cried. "Someone found him in his car and called the police."

"Aunt Inga," Alicia murmured. "Sit down and I'll make you some tea."

"I don't want any tea I want to see my boyfriend. I can't believe he would get himself killed now of all times!" But she went back to her seat.

A uniformed woman stood up. "You are this lady's niece?" She asked.

"Yes, I'm Alicia Mueller," Alicia answered.

"I gather this woman lives here, alone?" She commented.

"Yes, she does some of the time when I'm out of town. As I was when she called me but I got here as soon as I could," Alicia said.

"Sheriff Harding called me. I'm from the Senior Care Offices and I see her as needing help."

Alicia stiffened. Oh hell, she thought, I need to keep her at home until I get that insurance. A few million dollars doesn't grow on trees! "When I'm at work I have a neighbor lady come over and make her meals and keep her company."

"Well, in that case, your aunt is lucky to still be able to enjoy her home!" The woman smiled at Alicia. "And she's also so lucky to have you. Now that you're present, I will tell Sheriff Harding he can speak to her." And she went outside.

Minutes later an officer came in and shooed the people who were standing around with Inga out of the room saying, "Leave your names and address with one of the deputies. I will want to talk to you all sometime later!" Alicia took a breath as this tall good-looking man came into the living room.

"I understand you are this lady's niece?" He asked and took a seat across the room in an easy chair.

"Yes, I'm Alicia Mueller." She commented taking Inga's hand.

"Do you own a gun?" He asked Inga.

"Oh no sir," Inga said, "Why, whatever for?"

"Well, did you shoot him?"

Inga shrank closer to Alicia. "Oh no--, but how could that happen, he just left here. We are going away today!" she cried.

"The man is dead!" he declared. "How long ago did he leave here?"

"Just a little while, we are getting ready to go. You see we are going to Las Vegas to get married today!"

Sheriff Harding shook his head and looked at Alicia saying helplessly, "I will need to take your aunt in for questioning soon Miss Mueller." As he went back outside, the Medical Examiner was just leaving in his black van carrying the body of Inga's boyfriend. A tow truck was pulling the man's sedan down to police headquarters as it was the murder vehicle.

And Inga Mueller looked around wondering why all this was going on now, just when she had to get ready for her wedding!

-24-

Lindy ended her night at Shirlee's Place with a promise of getting together with her girlfriend for lunch later in the week. And getting into the taxi, she was sure she saw that same man who wanted to buy her a Manhattan sitting in a darkened vehicle parked near a side exit. Heeding the advice of staying ahead of a possible stalker, as she got in the vehicle she asked the driver, "Will you watch that black SUV by the exit door there and see if it follows us please?" She didn't want to turn around and possibly alert him.

And after a few minutes the driver spoke, "Miss, I think that same vehicle is following us." And he sped around several blocks, and then said, "In fact I'm sure of it now!"

Oh damn, Lindy thought. I can't go home and let him know where I live. "Could you lose him for fifty bucks?" She asked. And the driver laughed and exclaimed, "Watch me!" And Lindy was thrust against the back of the taxi seat as he stepped on the gas. As they sailed out to the highway by the ocean it wasn't long before the taxi driver laughed and said, "We left him back there in the dust. Now do you want to go to your address?"

Back home, Lindy only turned on a small lamp in her bedroom as she undressed. Slipping the .38 in the pocket of a robe she went to each window and peeked out. Then went out to the lanai and checked the locks on the windows and doors. Seeing that everything was locked up tight she settled down on a couch in the lanai and lit a cigarette. Moonlight shimmered on the ocean and the rolling waves hummed an unending refrain.

How she loved the water, not that she swam in it or liked to be out on it. She remembered that time with Mario D'Agustino, way back when. She had been dating this handsome man who turned out to be a drug lord, and then she had been a witness when he had shot and killed a man and tossed the body in the ocean. Lindy shivered remembering the awful trial that followed, of being kidnapped and left in that forest to die, but then relieved finally, knowing Mario and his brother had been killed in a shoot-out.

Thinking over all the episodes of her life now as she sat in the dark, she made up her mind she would use the .38 for protection from now on. No way was anyone going to be able to hurt her ever again!

Not that she didn't love living by the ocean and her friends, but she needed a plan now to organize her days. And the same one crept back into her thoughts begging for acceptance. Well, why not now? She thought sitting there in the darkened lanai.

She had always loved the mysterious persona of a medium. But she worried, would her clairvoyance surface again after all this time? With that thought in mind she sat back and relaxed and concentrated on her breathing and then meditation. Soon she was able to envision herself as that personality again. With that picture in her thoughts she fell into a relaxing restful sleep only to awaken and find her way into her bedroom for the rest of the night.

She awoke with a purpose in mind and immediately found the telephone number of an old friend whom she knew would help her, who lived in Monterrey, Mexico.

"Lola Lang!" Margaret Ames the watercolor artist exclaimed. "Where ever the hell did you disappear to?"

"I'm sorry Rita." Lindy answered using her nick name. "I had an emergency back home and had to close up my house here in South Carolina."

"I worried about you my dear!" Rita scolded.

"Thank you, I had to take care of some business up there and then I decided to visit a friend!"

"Lola, I was in Hilton Head a while back. You know, I didn't even have your cell phone number or else I could have tracked you down!"

"Sorry." Lindy said apologetic again.

"Okay, consider yourself balled out. Now let's have lunch soon but what's up now?"

Lindy swallowed. "Rita, I want to start up my business again and I need you to spread the word for me to your friends here in Hilton Head."

"Lola, do you mean start up your clairvoyant predictions again?"

"Yes." Lindy answered.

"Of course, I can help, my dear. I always knew you had the gift, after you saved me from getting killed in that restaurant when that awful earthquake hit Monterrey last year. I'll put in a call now to my lovely dear friends there for you!"

"Thanks Rita. I'm going to put out my sign and start seeing them again here in my home." She didn't mention she'd have her .38 on her now.

"Okay, I know there's no one there in Hilton Head to help those poor souls and they need you my dear. I'll get in touch with my friends there that you're back, so be ready!" And they ended with promises to call each other again very soon. Within minutes Margaret Ames had alerted her friends in Hilton Head that their revered medium was back and ready to see her followers.

Lindy found her old sign with the name Lola Lang, Mystic and tacked it on the front door. And now later, that same day she answered her doorbell with the .38 tucked in a pocket, when young girl stood on her doorstep looking lost and sad.

"I heard you could help me," she said faintly and then started to sway. Lindy reached out for her and helped her inside to a chair in her living room and then hurriedly got a bottle of water for her from the refrigerator and some crackers in the kitchen.

Hurrying back to her first customer, Lindy urged her to take her time and sip the water and eat the crackers. As the young woman silently did as she was told, her dark eyes darted anxiously here and there around the room. Sensing her discomfort, Lindy busied herself with straightening books and things on the nearby coffee table and humming under her breath. After several minutes the woman blurted out, "I just need to tell someone this! You see in my dreams someone is trying to kill me!"

Lindy took her arm and gently led her further into her house and to the small book-filled room, the library she liked to call it and used for her meetings. She studied the young dark-haired woman. She looked to be in her late teens and couldn't weigh more than a hundred and five pounds. She wore a short pink sleeveless dress and flip flops on her bare feet and her toenails were painted a bright pink as well.

"What is your name?' Lindy asked.

She whispered, "Edie."

"Edie, do you recognize this person in your dream?" Lindy asked.

"No," she whispered again. "But sometimes I think it's my boyfriend. But then it can't be him, he loves me!"

Lindy had sat very still next to Edie in an easy chair and was holding her hand. And as this young woman talked chills spread down her back as she saw a picture in her head of a dark-skinned man standing over Edie with a knife in his hand. Lindy sat up abruptly and took both her hands.

"Edie, do you live with someone?" She asked urgently.

"Yes, I live with my mama, why?" Edie replied and wiped at her teary eyes with a tissue. Her face was ashen.

Lindy stood up and pulled Edie to her feet. "Because," she said hastily, "you need to leave and go away for a while! Listen to me, do not tell anyone where you're going except your mother, and I mean no one!"

"But I must tell my boyfriend!' She wailed.

"No, you must not tell him anything for now." Lindy whispered, "Do you have a relative you can visit for a while?"

"Well yes." Edie offered wiping her eyes again. And with that plan in mind, the woman tried bravely to smile. As she left Edie pressed a roll of bills into Lindy's hand saying "I will do it right now! Thank you, thank you!"

Lindy closed and locked the door after her and sank down in a nearby chair for a few minutes. It had been months since she had used her clairvoyance and now she found herself feeling uneasy. As she had closed the front door, she saw six more people lined up and waiting for her. She thought to herself, how do I know that the same guy that tried to follow me home last night won't try to get to me right here in my own house posing as a customer?

She dropped her head down on the back of a chair and closed her eyes realizing now, she would have to carry that damn gun at all times.

-25-

Jason Edward Edwards was thirty-three years old. He hadn't amounted to much in his life according to today's standards, but he had learned how to stay out of jail most of the time. He'd attempted to work at a job a few times and had married once when he had found a female who would put up with his lack of employment in exchange for a sexual relationship. She hadn't been too pretty but had a hell of a job and brought home a hefty paycheck. But all good things soon come to an end, and she packed up his meager belongings and sent him on his way. He didn't always have or even need a female in his life but it had helped to have a woman to cook and wash his clothes now and then.

Jason was born late in life to a couple of "straight laced bible thumpers" as they were called back then. John and Olga Edwards lived on a small farm in Wisconsin where they eked out a meager living by growing their fruits and vegetables, raising their own chickens, a prized pig for meat and a cow for milk. They mainly kept to themselves and weren't social with anyone around the area. Their old car could be heard chugging along on the gravel roads on the way to church at least several times a week. When their son came along, the church ladies decided to have a baby shower for them and gave them lovely handmade items. But after that the only times the little family ventured out with their precious child was to attend the lengthy sermons they found comfort in.

Jason quit school in the seventh grade when his dad became ill and passed away leaving him to take care of his mother and failing that, his mother too passed. It didn't take long for seventeen-year old Jason Edwards to strike out leaving the meager little farm in the north to wither and die. He traveled to California and was awed by the evergreen landscape, and the ocean. Then he crossed the country to the east. This took him many years but he finally settled in the western states and then called Billings, Montana his home. Here he found the high heeled Western boots added inches to his five-foot five frame. And when he added one of his Western hats he saw himself as a tall bad ass.

He'd gotten lucky in a card game a while back, and with a couple of grand stuffed in his pocket, he had a plan in mind. A friggin' good one he'd dreamed about for years, and now Jason searched for a place to start his venture. He soon found an abandoned run-down farm on the outskirts of Billings, and after not seeing any neighboring residents he drove in. This would be the perfect place to put his plan into action. Hiding his pickup behind some out buildings and using his tools he pried open the door to the house and then the huge barn. Both places were full of junk and old furniture but he moved his few bags of belongings in and got to work.

It had taken time to get supplies in the outlying towns and get started but using growing lights in the big old barn he soon had a crop of weed growing tall behind covered windows. He had rigged up hoses for watering and every night he would carefully mist the plants. And, he had bought a dog that he kept outside in a small enclosure in case someone tried to snoop around.

Now he was a farmer with thousands of dollars invested in his crop. And in just a few more weeks the plants would be ready to cut and dry, and then he could package it and get rich. The dollar signs blinded him. The only thing that niggled in the back of his mind was that goddamned accident he was in a while back. Maybe he would be found guilty of driving drunk, but he would be packed and long gone before anything would come of that!

He had never seen the woman the night of that accident when he'd come to still sitting in his smashed pickup. Sure, he had way too many beers and was driving blind drunk but it was late and the streets should have been clear so what the hell was this old bat doing out anyway?

Jason had bought a pizza and a quart of milk to bring home for his supper and was sitting among the junk filled area that had been a living room in its day when the dog started barking. He jumped up. There were no curtains on the windows but old shades hung crookedly on the two that looked out to the yard.

Sure enough, that same dude was back that he'd met earlier. Reed something from the insurance company, Jason remembered. What the hell—, what the hell was he snooping around for? Jason watched as he came right up to the house and looked in the windows. God damned if he didn't come right up to the one he was standing by. Jason ducked down and his heart pumped hard. Could the fucker smell the pizza, he wondered? He listened as the asshole must have gone to every window in the house. Then he dared peek out when he heard receding steps and he saw the guy apparently giving up and leaving.

Jason ate the pizza and guzzled the milk. He didn't dare light a cigarette in case the dude came back as the smell would drift out into the yard. And he didn't dare go outside in case the guy was watching so he stretched out on his bed roll and caught a nap. As was his habit, he'd awake at around two a.m. and go out to the barn and take care of his plants. Months ago, he'd bought those packs of seeds from over the internet and had patiently filled hundreds of growing pots with fertilized planting soil. Then sat back, and sure enough the seeds began to sprout. There were hundreds of gorgeous little green seedlings that looked like dollar bills to him. Rows and rows of them and he'd nursed them into hip-high, tall healthy plants.

When he got back in the house after their nightly misting, tightness began to grow in his belly as he tried to sleep. A goddamned crawling uneasiness in his gut he'd grown to realize meant trouble was coming. And Jesus, right now, he had too much going to ignore it!

He went back out to the barn that night and turned the fans he'd bought on high to dry the plants out and then the next day got started cutting and spreading them on the canvasses to dry. He had wanted to wait a few more weeks to increase their height as that meant more cash. But like a farmer hearing a prediction of bad weather, he would work like hell now to get out of there fast. It would take a few days!

-26-

Reed Conners went back to the restaurant at his hotel in Billings where he downed a straight shot of Crown Royal and then ate a steak at the bar in the dining room. He'd gotten to know the bartender and now she leaned over the bar and planted a kiss right on his lips. And again, he couldn't help but notice the plunging neckline in her shirt as she did.

"Hmm-, now that's the correct way to greet your customer." Reed grinned

She laughed "You looked like you needed some cheering up my friend!"

"Maybe so." Reed commented. "My day hasn't been that productive, seems like I'm just spinning my wheels."

"Anything I can help you with Reed?" She asked and winked at him with a provocative twinkle in her brown eyes.

"Of course, you could. What are you doing after closing?" Reed asked playing along.

"I'm not sure," she said.

"Well can you leave early?" Reed asked. "Is the boss around, maybe I could talk him into letting you off."

She leaned over the bar again. "Sorry I can't do that, you see I'm the boss!"

Reed sat up straighter on the stool. "You mean I just got a kiss from the owner of this joint?"

"Absolutely." She joked.

"I must be special then!" Reed commented. And they went on playfully bantering back and forth throughout the night. At midnight, Reed got up off the bar to leave, and she came back over and whispered, "Do you want company tonight?"

"If it's you, sure." He answered. "Room number 210."

"I know," she answered, "I checked earlier."

"Really," Reed grinned as his day was looking better.

Not surprising, the Billings Hotel had a Western décor of mustached old settlers in framed pictures, and assorted lasso's, guns and hats all attached to the walls which continued into the dining room. Even old-time tunes rolled out of the hidden speakers, and

Reed recognized some of the oldies. It was fine for a while then thankfully the bartender had switched to everyday country.

Carrie Underwood was singing her latest "You'll Never Know," from her new album as Reed got in the elevator for his floor.

Goddamn he growled, he had been able to spend most of the night not thinking of Lindy. What the hell good did it do now anyway? She had made her choice and left. And he would get over her just like she seems to be getting over him, so to hell with her! He was moving on too!

Back in his room, he quickly showered and put on fresh clothes, then sat down and turned the television on to the late show. He got up when he heard a soft knock on his door, and there stood the gorgeous woman with a bottle of Crown Royal, ice and glasses on a tray.

"Room service," she said smiling and coming in and setting the tray on a table.

"Just in time," Reed commented, "I was getting thirsty!"

"Well, I like to keep my customers well taken care of even after hours!" Julie said and laughed. "Reed, I take it I'm not keeping you up!"

"Nope, I'm good!"

"You're in town on business I gather?" She went on as she filled their glasses and handed him one, then took a seat in a chair that belonged to the writing desk.

"I do investigating for an insurance company and am here on a case." Reed said as he tasted the drink.

"You said you're from Minnesota?" Julie had sat down and slipped off her boots, in her case they were low heeled.

"From the northern part." He added. "I've been in this area elk hunting over the years so I'm somewhat familiar with the country."

"I've been to Minneapolis a number of times to shop and then to attend different functions. And then of course, to the Mall of America once or twice."

They went on talking for a while then Reed got up and pulled her into his arms. At first, she felt different then Lindy's familiar curves, and he faltered, but he determinedly shut off his thoughts of Lindy and went on. He brought his lips to hers and tasted her again, then proceeded to her neck and down her neckline and then she stepped back.

Oh damn, he thought as he looked in her eyes. A tease!

But she saved the day when she whispered, "Let's get comfy," and pulled the covers down on the bed and turned the lamp on low which stood on a table. Before he knew what was happening she stood without a stitch of clothes on saying, "Give me five minutes in the shower and I'll join you there," and she was gone!

Well, Reed grinned, just a little bit drunk by now and said to the room, "I like where this is going!" And he settled into the king-sized bed leaning back against the pillows. He brushed his hair off his forehead and tucked the gray sides behind his ears. Then wondered if his Calvin Klein plaid boxers were too loud for someone his age.

Well hell, he thought. Enjoy it old man. Who knows when you'll get lucky like this again! Then Julie came out of the shower all pink and smelling good. And as she slipped into bed, Reed could feel her nipples against his chest.

He pulled her down on top and took one in his mouth and suckled, then the other as she raised up and gave him room to do it without smothering him in the fullness of her breasts. Then he slid on top and began planting kisses on her belly, her thighs and when he found her secret place with his tongue she cried out in ecstasy. When he entered her, she moaned and lay relaxed and whispered his name. Time sped by and then, they lay entwined together as their bodies cooled.

"Well, Mr. Investigator." Julie said then "you sure found me out!" Then sat up and pulled the sheet over them and lay back down in his arms.

"However, I need to get out of here shortly," She murmured then, "But I could go for a quickie if you're up for it!"

Reed grinned and agreed. A streetlight outside sent a glow up into the room and he vaguely remembered her untangling herself from his embrace and leaving his bed later in the night.

It was early morning when Reed got to Inga Mueller's house the next day. As he stood on the cement steps knocking on the front door, he could hear a radio blasting a rock and roll song by the Beatles. He knocked again louder this time and called out, "Is anyone home?"

"Yes, yes, hold your horse's young man," And Inga came to the screen door and looked out. "I remember you, that insurance man!" She exclaimed. "When are you going to fix my car, I need it mister!" She raised a fist at him.

She stood there in a red robe of faded chenille. Her gray tangled hair was hanging loose from the bun she'd had before when he'd met her. Today she looked her age which was seventy-nine as listed in the file.

"Hello Mrs. Mueller," Reed said, "May I come in?"

She stood there unsure of what to do, then remarked, "Why?" And she didn't move.

"Who is it?" Reed could hear another woman asking as she approached. And then her niece, Alicia Mueller stood there.

"What is it you might need now?" She asked through the screen not inviting him in.

Reed introduced himself to Alicia and then commented, "I just need a clearer picture of what happened the night of the car accident."

Alicia put a protective arm around her aunt. "Oh no, can't you see she's in no shape to go through that again!"

"But I need my car fixed up," Inga protested pulling away. "Can't you remember, my boyfriend and I are driving to Vegas to get married today!" Inga looked at Alicia, then at Reed.

Alicia shook her head. "Mr. Conners, she's in no shape to see anyone now!" She moved away from the screen door and attempted to close the main door. Reed stepped back but as he did the high collar on her shirt slipped down and he saw the birth mark. The very same wine colored one that covered her lower cheek and down her neck he remembered seeing on that stripper in a bar downtown awhile back, they'd called her CeCe. What the hell?

He left then and instead of driving away, he stopped in the next block and parked and started knocking on doors. Sometimes he just had to get out and talk to the people surrounding a case. There were a couple things he needed to have verified, and that was first of all, did Inga Mueller actually drive that old Buick she was so worried about? And did she have a memory problem?

Most of the people were gone or didn't answer their door, but as Reed ended up at a house behind the Mueller residence where their garages met in the alley, he ran in to an old man just parking his car. A straw hat sat jauntily on his head and his face crinkled up in a toothless smile when he greeted Reed and exclaimed about the nice day. When Reed asked if he had seen Inga Mueller drive lately, he laughed and said, "Nah, she gave that up years ago when they said she was a little daft," and he circled a finger, "But that niece of hers does when she's here." He laughed then and winked, "Alicia says she works at a bank, but I heard different if you know what I mean."

-27-

Lindy loved being back in her house in Hilton Head, SC. It was a three-bedroom, three bath rambler with a library and a lanai that faced the rolling waters of the Atlantic Ocean. She had just made a killing on her investments when she purchased the property. At the time, prices had been low and the future looked pretty dismal for this small island, but then suddenly it took off when word of the bargain prices got out. People grabbed up the real estate and the trend started upward. Now it was again a thriving island of rich hotels, businesses and tourists.

She had spent time and money making the place into something that incited both her wishes and her imagination. She had worked with Journey, an innovative decorator who dressed like a man but talked like a girl. And between the two of them it turned out to be a showplace. The colors of light sage and a soft blue mixed with cream were used throughout; in the window coverings, in the rugs over the light wooden floors and in the furnishings. And now it was a beautiful backdrop to the blue waters of the ocean just outside.

Lindy felt rested as she showered and dressed for the day. Dammit she was not going to let the thought of some weirdo who was wandering the island get in her way of her life. But just in case she slid the .38 in the pocket of her white trousers and slipped a shirt over to cover the bulge. She gelled her wet short blonde hair and tousled it. Then stuck her tongue out at her reflection in the mirror and laughed as she had learned to do each day. Then whispered her usual mantra, Lindy, you still look dam good! Back in the kitchen then for another cup of coffee before it was time to see if she had any customers waiting outside needing her help this morning.

Her cell rang out a short rendition of America the Beautiful and when she picked up Louie Lui, the owner of that swanky hotel in Minneapolis was on the other end

"Lola Lang, I'm so glad I found you!"

"Louie, it's been awhile. How are you?" Lindy exclaimed.

"I'm fine Lola, listen I'm attending an event down here, right in your town and thought I'd call and see if you would like to show off your city to me."

Lindy smiled into the phone remembering the lovely time she'd had when she stopped in at his place on her way out of Minnesota some time ago. But that was before she'd been kidnapped and raped. "Why Louie, I'd love too. Where are you staying?" She asked.

"I'm at the Hilton Inn right on Main Street and 5th Avenue," He told her.

"Lovely place," Lindy said.

"Well, I'll look forward to seeing you again." Louie remarked. "Are you driving or should I come by and get you?" He asked.

"I'll pick you up. I just got a blue Mercedes and I'll wait at the door for you."

"Hmm-, can't say I've been picked up for quite a while now, but I'll be watching for you!" Louie joked.

Then Lindy called Shirlee's Place and reserved a table for two at 7:15. "I would like a bottle of your best champagne chilling at the table too," She ordered.

Her day took on a vibe of excitement, but she had to calm down and concentrate as now when she peeked out her window she saw several people patiently waiting her welcome. And opening her door she saw two young women and one elderly man sitting comfortably in the chaise lounge chairs she had set up out there on the patio for her people.

The beads on her shirt sparkled in the morning sun as she stepped out. "Good morning friends," she said. "Now who will be my first lovely person today?" And one of the women stood up and Lindy smiled at her. "Follow me," she said and they went in and she shut the door.

"Can I help you with something today?" she asked when they were seated in the library.

The woman looked to be in her early twenties. A tall, thin, beautiful brunette. Her eyes were dark and her skin was tanned, and she wore no make-up. She had on black shorts and a white t-shirt. She sat down and nervously picked at her lip.

"My mother said maybe you could." She looked around the room nervously, at the rows of books on the shelves.

"Okay, I'll try," Lindy said and took her hand. "May I ask your name?"

"It's Mia."

"What do you need Mia?"

She took a shaky breath and said hesitatingly, "My fiancé would kill me if he knew I was talking to an outsider, but I need to know if I should marry him. You see I think my boyfriend is involved in the drug world!" She picked again at her lip.

As soon as Lindy heard her say "the drug world" her blood ran cold remembering that the infamous

D'Agustino family had its long arm spread over some of the island, although some of the leaders were now dead. Mia felt the tremor in Lindy's hand and she drew back. But Lindy hastily regrouped her thoughts and smiled.

My dear Mia," she then said carefully. "I guess you have to decide what kind of life you want."

"I love him so." Mia went on to say holding back tears.

Mia, if you have doubts you must resolve them now, not later!" Lindy commented carefully.

The young woman sat for a minute quietly and then springing up before Lindy could continue, said, "I know exactly what I have to do! Thank you!" She pressed some bills in Lindy's hand and rushed out of the house.

Lindy had to take a few minutes to calm her nerves after this episode. This was the first time anyone had come to her with that problem. And she had to be very careful. If word got out she was deliberately attacking the drug family in some way, she would be quickly silenced. And she was not going to give up her life and her island home because of them. She sucked in her breath and with her hand on the .38 in her trouser pocket stepped out on her patio for her next customer and the afternoon continued as she helped her following find comfort.

At the end of the day, she had a pile of bills to add to her growing bank deposit. Life was good!

She ran a tub and added bubble bath to the water and thankfully sank in. And Lordy, it felt good! She put her head back on the bath pillow and thought about Louie. Hmm- would she sleep with him this time? He was handsome and rich and he made her feel wonderful. Maybe this time she would allow him into her life here on the island and bring him home with her.

-28-

"But where is my boyfriend?" Inga whispered again as Alicia spread a blanket over her aunt as she lay in her bed upstairs. She had talked the police officer into letting Inga rest for an hour before bringing her down to the police station.

Earlier that morning someone had heard shots coming from somewhere in Inga's neighborhood and called it in. And after investigating in the area the police had found a man, dead in his car in the driveway right outside her home. By the time Alicia got there it was close to noon, and Inga was sitting at the kitchen table wringing her hands as strangers were milling around trying to get her to talk.

"What the hell is going on," Alicia barked to the people, barging in on the scene. "Can't you see, my aunt is in no condition for this!"

"We need to know what went on here," a gruff voiced detective claimed stepping closer.

Inga ran to her and Alicia had put her arms around her as she said tearfully. "They say my boyfriend is gone. But they won't tell me where, and they keep asking if I shot him?"

"Shh- Aunt Inga, it's okay."

"Shot him they say but I don't even have a gun," she protested.

And that's when the two women went upstairs, and Alicia coaxed her to lie down and rest. After a few minutes Inga was snoring gently and Alicia went downstairs to see if she could straighten out the madhouse. Reed Conners had been standing in the living room and came over to her as she picked up newspapers and empty paper coffee cups from the table and cupboard.

"Could I have a word with you Miss Mueller?" He asked.

"Conners, what are you after? You can see that the damn accident has caused my aunt to become totally unglued!"

"Has she been like this before?" He asked.

"She has always been alert and able to lead a pretty normal life."

"I'm wondering where she got the idea to sue my insurance company." Reed asked then.

"Who knows." Alicia exclaimed.

"I'll need to get her doctors name, and of course her attorney," He commented dryly.

Alicia sucked in her breath and willed her own nerves to quiet as she walked him to the door.

And then suddenly Reed Conners turned to her and said, "Miss Mueller I saw you in a lingerie show the other day. You go by the name CeCe?"

"Me? No, that's not me!" Alicia exclaimed momentarily unnerved.

"Miss Mueller, I see that same birth mark on the side of your face and neck just now as this CeCe had! Same one! Why are you denying you are one and the same?"

Alicia's face paled, he knew! But knew exactly what? "Okay," she confessed, "It's just that I don't want anyone to know what I do for a living."

Reed just looked at her and shook his head.

"Well, I don't want my dear, sweet aunt to know Mr. Conners. Since getting hit by that irresponsible jerk, she's had a very hard time with everyday life and is becoming more and more unstable and not able to take care of herself. She's so bad now, she needs to go into one of those assisted living places and that costs money!"

"Well, I agree it's costly. But there are agencies that can help you know." Reed mentioned.

"Sure, but she's very proud. She'd never take any handouts! And she wants that Edwards man to pay for what he did to her!"

Reed commented, "The police chief says she's been unresponsive to any of his questions this morning. Has she said anything at all to you?" Reed asked.

"Only that she doesn't have a gun and 'why hasn't her boyfriend come over?" Alicia remarked. "She needs to rest and I need to get all these people out of here, look at them just like a bunch of god-damned vultures picking through her things!" Alicia announced, "Everyone out, if you want to know something, I'll meet you outside!"

And within minutes the house was cleared. However, outside the neighbors had come over to stare along with the news people from local TV stations.

Alicia Mueller was totally unnerved by it all, as a blonde TV announcer called over amid the whispering crowd, "Did that woman shoot her boyfriend? I heard it was a lover's quarrel between those old people!"

Hell, Alicia's thoughts scrambled, just what had she gotten herself into?

-29-

Lindy Lewis, aka Lola Lang put the top down on her new Mercedes convertible and took off down the street from her house on Hilton Head Island. Her blonde hair was gelled to perfection and looked even sexier after the wind had ruffled it, as she drove on her way to pick up Louie Lui at the Hilton Inn for their date. She glanced up in the visor mirror to check her teeth and was satisfied that they gleamed pearly white. Her little black dress had a low neckline and was sleeveless and short, and by now she had acquired a nice golden tan from her walks on the beach and felt like a million.

She had met Louie that first night in Minneapolis and he had shown her an enjoyable evening with a lovely dinner at a beautiful restaurant and they had ended the night on a friendly note.

She didn't know much about Louie yet except that he was from London and apparently was a well-known architect and builder there. He had regaled her with his experiences in Minneapolis, a new city, let alone a new country. Although he had traveled to the U.S. numerous times in the past and had attended college here, it was entirely different for a non-resident to start a business here.

She cruised up to the front door of the elite hotel in Hilton Head and stopped where a valet hurried over and opened her car door as Louie slid in.

"Hello handsome," Lindy exclaimed and smiled.

"Hi gorgeous." He said as he slid into the blue leather seat of her Mercedes.

Lindy gave him a once over quickly and smiled. Damn, he was looking good and dressed casually in beige linen trousers and a cocoa brown shirt. His hair was dark brown with gray mingled around his temples and his eyes were just as dark as she remembered and held a slight hint of an Asian ancestry.

"How do you like my island so far?" She asked.

"This is absolutely stunning Lindy," Louie answered. "As I said, I've never traveled here to the Carolina's before. The foliage is breathtaking!"

"That's what I love about living here, seeing the palm trees and then the Spanish moss adorning our wonderful old oaks!"

"For someone like me, coming from foggy old England, I love it." Louie commented as he slipped on a pair of Prada sun glasses.

They were driving along the ocean's highway to the downtown area where Lindy's friend Shirlee had her nightclub. The sun was making its slow decline in the west and it turned the skies into a rainbow of breathtaking colors.

Within a few minutes they had parked and as they came into the restaurant a tall good-looking man in a tux greeted them.

"Hello Jordy, we have a reservation under my name." Lindy said.

"Yes, I have a good table for you and your guest tonight. Follow me please."

Louie Lui held her arm as they dodged tables and busy waiters to a perfect corner table that overlooked the water on one side and was next to the entertainment, which of course was Shirlee at her Baby Grand tantalizing people with romantic medleys.

After getting settled with champagne cocktails Lindy winked at her pal Shirlee who smiled back at her and raised a questionable eyebrow apparently about her handsome date. Louie reached for her hand from across the table as Shirlee sang the love song, "I Left My Heart in San Francisco."

"Let me order for us tonight Lola. You do like seafood, don't you?" He asked later after several cocktails."

"I do, except anything with escargot!" She laughed and wrinkled her nose. The dance floor across the room became crowded as Shirlee brought out an always good-old song called the "Tennessee Waltz" that had an easy beat. And after Louie had placed their dinner order they got up to dance.

As Louie took her in his arms and she felt his hard and trim body next to hers, she took in a breath. She thought of Reed and compared their builds and for a minute she felt lonely and blue. But darn it, she didn't want to spoil her evening yearning over their lost love. And she laid her head on Louie's shoulder and joined him step for step in the dance. After lingering on the dance floor and a few words of greetings with Shirlee as Lindy introduced Louie, they returned to their seats just as their waiter arrived with a loaded tray of goodies. There were crab cakes with a creamy Mediterranean salsa, flame broiled lobster and roasted green and gold veggies. And a bottle of Santa Margherita wine to go with the delicious dinner.

"Yumm-" Lindy murmured as the waiter put a napkin around her neck and did the same for Louie. "Do you want me to shell the lobster for you?" He asked.

"Yes please." Louie replied after Lindy shook her head. "Okay here's to us," he said and they raised their glasses in a toast.

Sometime later, Shirlee finished her set and came over as they were sipping a liqueur with their coffee. Then Louie excused himself to check on something, he said.

"Pretty impressive huh?" Lindy said grinning at her friend.

"Well yeah, but why is he calling you Lola?" Shirlee asked with a puzzled look on her face.

Lindy winked at her friend. "Well, it's a long story but I'll bring you up to date some time."

"I hope soon, Lola/Lindy or I'll just assume you're hiding out for some reason!" Shirlee laughed.

"Who me?" Lindy just smiled at her friend. But she did feel almost criminal caught in this lie that had started way back in Minneapolis when she'd met Louie. Tomorrow she'd call Shirlee and explain.

Louie came back then. "What did I miss?" he asked pulling out his chair to sit.

"You'd be surprised," Lindy laughed and blew him a kiss.

"I know you're from across the pond Louie, so how do you like us?" Shirlee asked.

"Much too crass, according to my mum, who is still perky at ninety-three." He laughed and went on, "But for me, I like you all just fine." Louie answered and leaned over and tipped Lindy's lips to his.

"Louie is a builder Shirlee, he's just finished a lavish one hundred room hotel in Minneapolis!" Lindy remarked.

"Really! How wonderful, are you here now for a vacation?" She asked.

"And more," he grinned. "I have some meetings and a conference here. And, I hope to get in some golf while here in the sunny south."

Shirlee checked her watch and stood then. "I've got to get back, my friends. Any requests?" she asked.

"Yes," Lindy said and smiled, "Would you do 'Crazy' by Patsy Cline?" she asked.

"Of course, that's one of my favorite songs." Shirlee said and left their table. And soon the room was hushed as she was back at her piano.

Lindy and Louie spent the rest of the evening dancing and sipping on a magnificent liqueur. At the end of the evening seeing Lindy had drunk too much to drive, he took the keys to her Mercedes and drove back to his hotel.

At the door he stopped and gave the keys to a valet and helped her out saying, "You're coming in with me Lola, and I want you to stay awhile." And before she knew it she was sitting in his suite admiring the architecture. He joined her on the couch and they kissed. A long hot, deep one that made them both catch their breath. That was when he picked her up and carried her to the bedroom and began to undress her after he sat her down on the edge of the king-sized bed. He slid her feet out of her high heeled sandals then unzipped her little black dress and pulled it down over her waist. After slipping it off over her ankles he laid her down on the pillows.

Now she was glad she had shopped for the new lingerie while in Minneapolis, it had cost a fortune but it was an investment in feeling sexy again. A necessity she needed, she smiled inwardly in her inebriated state.

She awoke early the next morning and for a moment couldn't remember where she was. When she glanced over and saw this stranger sleeping soundly on the next pillow, she almost shrieked. Then he reached for her and murmured her name and she suddenly remembered the night before and almost blushed recalling her actions.

Lordy, had she really done those things with him, she worried? Now this morning she felt an enormous headache edging its way in and claiming her thoughts.

She sat up and brushed her hair off her face saying, "Louie, my love as much as I like this, I have to get home and rush off to a meeting!"

"No, you can't go right now," He whispered, "Stay Lola and we'll order room service for breakfast!"

"I wish I could, my handsome sweetheart, but I have to go. Maybe next time!" And she kissed him quickly, gathered her clothes and hurried into the bathroom for a quick shower. She brushed her wet blond tresses, applied a hint of make-up and was out in twenty minutes.

Louie was lounging in bed reading a newspaper when she came out.

"Sure, you won't join me for coffee?" he asked lowering it and smiling. "Hmm- you look pretty hot this morning Lola!"

"Thanks Louie, I'd love to later. I've had a wonderful time, but I have important meetings today!" Of course, he was unaware that the real reason was that she had a business to get back to.

"Would you call for my car please?"

She blew him a kiss then as within minutes the concierge knocked on the door and offered his arm and assistance to the elevator, and then outside to where a valet stood ready with her Mercedes.

Lordy, she thought again, I really could get used to all this!

A short time later she drove into the driveway she was totally unaware of the nondescript sedan that had been following her as it just casually sped on by.

-30

Alicia Mueller was so tired of being around her loony aunt, as she thought of her. She just had to get out and, on the road, again to save her own sanity. For Christ's sake, she had just shot and killed a man! She didn't feel any remorse as she hadn't had a choice, she argued with herself. That asshole had filled her befuddled aunt with sweet words and marriage only to get that insurance money when it came through. And of course, her aunt had been giddy at the thought that she was going to be a bride.

When Alicia thought about it, she hadn't even known the man's name only that he was a neighbor who had been licking at Inga's skirts. And Inga had admitted telling him about her windfall of millions of dollars soon to be coming. Of course, her aunt didn't understand that she had been tricked by her niece, that she had not been in the car when Jason Edwards ran into her as she was making that left turn. Or that Alicia was really the driver, and that she and Jason were both drunk! He was too drunk to remember exactly what happened and so was she. But being the cunning person Alicia was, she needed to stick around just a little longer here in Billings until the investigations in the accident were safely done with.

She had stayed in bed until noon as was her usual habit and today the little house in the rundown neighborhood was silent, which was not usual for this time of the day. Inga's habit was to have both her old-style televisions blaring and a radio or two on as well. Alicia got out of bed and looked around the house for her aunt. But Inga wasn't anywhere in the house. Damn, Alicia grumbled. Now she had to get dressed and go and look for her as sometimes she wondered off.

Alicia threw on a pair of jeans and a sweatshirt, and slipped on her boots, then opened the door. The autumn day was warm but cloudy, and a mist fell over the landscape. The area had many mature trees but now the leaves were all down leaving the branches barren. In its day, the neighborhood would have been quite lovely with young families and clipped lawns but it had gone downhill as kids grew and moved away. Now mostly only the old folks were left.

At the back of the lot was a scrubby piece of land that in its day had held lovely flower and vegetable gardens, but today it stood filled with weeds. And here was where she found Inga.

"What the hell are you doing out here, for cripes sake it raining!" Alicia said crossly. "I've been looking all over for you!"

Inga had taken a small stool out to the middle of the patch and was busily pulling weeds. The mist glistened in her gray hair and her t-shirt clung to her wet bra-less shape.

"Alicia look, I'm getting this ready for my plants again!" And Inga excitedly waved a hand over the weed filled area.

"Oh, for God's sake," Alicia groaned. "It's been years since anything has been planted and grown in there. Inga it's raining, you need to come inside and change into dry clothes." Alicia said very patiently.

"Not yet, you see I need to get everything planted before we leave on our honeymoon!" She looked off in the distance and smiled. And said shyly, "It might be awhile before I can get away to tend to this!"

"Listen, dammit, you need to come with me right now." Alicia said gruffly. And after more threats, finally, Inga got up and followed Alicia into the house. Minutes later, the front doorbell rang and Inga ran to it excitedly saying, "That's him, I'll tell him it'll just be a minute while I change my dress!" She opened the door to two strangers.

"Are you Inga Mueller?" A tall dark-haired man asked.

"What--," was all Inga could muster in confusion after seeing it was not her boyfriend.

Alicia hurried to the door then, and shooed Inga away. "And who are you?" She asked.

"We're from the State Crime Bureau here in Montana." And they showed their badges. "We know the sheriff took down all the information about the shooting, and we don't want to inconvenience you lovely ladies, but we need to talk to Inga Mueller please."

"I'm her niece, what may I ask about?" Alicia stood in front of Inga hopefully to stem anything she might volunteer.

"We're investigating the shooting. May we come in?"

Ah-- Christ, Alicia thought. How the hell am I going to keep her quiet! "It might be better to do this another time I need to help her get cleaned up!" But then Inga stepped forward, dripping wet and muddy and said happily, "I'm Inga Mueller and I'm getting my garden ready for planting before I go on my honeymoon!"

The two men looked at her and then at each other, not sure if this was a joke or what.

"Inga," Alicia quickly stepped in and said, "Go get out of those clothes and for God's sake, get in the shower!" She tried hard to keep the bitchiness out of her voice.

After Inga had left the room she looked at the officers to gain their reaction, but they still had the same stony look on their faces.

"We understand the shooting of the victim took place on this property!" The shorter of the two men said.

"That's right." Alicia said.

"What was he doing here, did Mrs. Mueller know him?" He continued looking at his notes.

"I don't know." Alicia commented.

"Well, we understand that he lived right here in the neighborhood.'" He went on.

Alicia laughed, "You've met her, how would she know, she isn't well!"

"Has she seen a doctor?" The taller of the two stepped in and asked "I see she has got an insurance claim going on."

Alicia didn't answer.

"Was she hurt in that accident?" He wanted to know.

"Gentlemen, you have seen the results. Now if you'll excuse me, I need to see to my dear aunt!"

"When can we talk to her directly?" they persisted.

"She's been through enough," Alicia left them standing by the door saying over her shoulder; "You can see yourselves out!"

When she came in to the bathroom, Inga was still standing in her wet clothes, rolling her dusty hair in sponge curlers.

Alicia took a deep breath to steady her nerves and not shout at the woman! She'd go nuts herself if she had to stay around any longer! And then she said, "Listen, I need to go back to work for a few days, I'm calling the lady next door to stay with you. Now take a shower and go to bed!"

Alicia left orders with her to not let anyone in to talk to Inga, no matter what! Then she got in her rented car and got the hell away, not noticing that the same two men were already knocking on doors around the neighborhood.

She caught up with her group at a place called "Sheer Delight" in Grand Forks which was a huge barn like structure on the edge of town. They had several standard dates through-out the area that drew hundreds of males and some women, for miles around. Marianne was back with them here and the four girls put on a show that could make any red-blooded guy blush. Sometimes at the end of the night when the curtain went down, lacy G-strings would fly through the air to be caught by the lusty men, not sure that in the frenzy if they had actually seen the women slide the G-strings down over their hips. It was only a gimmick that Clark the owner and driver had come up with and had bought up a huge box of these treasures!

Audrey, Mary and Diane were sitting in the back seat of the limo as Alicia climbed in. "Christ ladies give me some room!" She bitched to her good friends that first night back, as they were on their way back to their rooms after the best night ever. Each one had hastily put their rolls of bills in their bras, the safest place before leaving the giant-sized barn.

"Good to have you back, CeCe," little Mary offered. "Oh sure, now we have to share our cash with her!" Audrey said good naturally as they all adjusted in their seats in the limo.

"Well, she sure cut into my money," Diane griped.

"Well, fuck you all then, I can go out on my own if that's how you feel!" Alicia shot back.

"Ah--, shut up all of you, or I'll leave you all in this shit town and go back to New York where I can make a lot more dough working with someone who appreciates me and what I do for them!" And that did shut them up as they realized without Clark to drive them around and book their dates and rooms, they would be lost.

"Clarky baby, we're sorry, we'll make it up to you." They all chimed in to say, and the rest of the night everyone was quiet, each one probably realizing how easy they really had it.

Several days went by and autumn was quickly fading into brisk gray days when Alicia got a call from the lady who was helping Inga. On this particular day,

Inga wasn't there when she went to fix her breakfast, and her bed didn't look like she had slept in it either!

"What the hell?" Alicia swore things had been going along so smoothly. She was just waiting to hear the court date from the lawyer, who she had checked with a week ago, for her aunt of course!

"What should I do?" The woman wanted to know.

Alicia was still with her troupe and was hundreds of miles away from Billings, Montana. She couldn't just run out and be there shortly.

"Goddammit," she exclaimed. "When was the last time you saw her?"

"She was fine last evening when I took her supper over. I had made her favorite chicken and dumplings!"

"Did you stay to see her eat it?" Alicia asked.

"Well, no but it was gone this morning!"

"Okay, here's what you need to do. Search the entire house, the yard, and the shed for her. I'll call you back in a few hours. She's got to be around there somewhere!" And Alicia went back to bed.

-31-

Reed Conners woke up in a bad mood. He had spent too much time in this cowboy town. By now he should have had this case wrapped up with a decision. His cell rang then and damn it all, it was his boss from Federated Insurance calling.

"Conners, what the hell is going on, you should have had this shit-sized claim figured out by now?" The man's voice boomed over the air waves.

Not letting the boss's agitation get to him, Reed said, "Yeah, I've run into some issues. But I'll have it in a day or two!"

"Make it soon. I've got another humongous claim coming in. And I need you back here yesterday!"

Actually, the insurance company handled all forms of coverage on cars, homes, lives and businesses and this small claim was peanuts compared to most. But the boss hated giving out his money as he called it, unless he had absolutely no choice and that's where Reed came in. However, Reed made a percentage when a case was settled, either way.

This case that Inga Mueller had suing Jason Edwards was for five million claiming negligence while under the influence causing her bodily harm. And goddammit he was going to settle it today!

He had met and interviewed the claimant, Inga Mueller, and her doctor had explained she was definitely in the early stages of dementia. That it was a disease that lent itself to many different avenues in which to express itself. And that a patient could possibly endure many years of living with it before having to be hospitalized and cared for by professionals.

Inga Mueller admitted she must have been driving that night but couldn't remember. But the poor woman couldn't remember what she did yesterday! And then there was the niece, a stripper! She certainly was a strange one. What the hell was her story? When he'd told her, he recognized her as being one of the strippers in the bar he'd stopped in at one evening, she first tried to deny it. Then claimed she hid her profession because she didn't want it known what she did for a living. Really, who gave a damn in this day and age anyway, but "wackiness seemed to run in the family," Reed grumbled. Now, granted Inga Mueller seemed to have "gone around the bend" but she did have the presence of mind to contact an attorney and want to sue for a huge sum of money. He had to get to the bottom of this damn case and get back home. His boat was still out and God knows when the snowstorm predicted for next week would reach his place in Minnesota.

And he had to find out what the hell Jason's story was. He was the insured, and he should have counter sued. But Jason claimed he wasn't interested. What the hell was that really about? The last few times when Reed had driven to his place, it looked the same, run-down and forlorn. The man was never home and whenever Reed had stopped and got out of his car at the gate, that damn dog always jumped up and ran over growling and showing his teeth.

The man was gone every day and most evenings. And the sheriff had not gotten back to him about this guy. Was he a renter or a squatter?

Reed was still in a bad mood that evening, and goddammit he was going to get to the bottom of this twisted case. He stopped at a grocery store and picked up some ground beef and over-the-counter Benadryl pills, then made a large meatball out of the ground beef and stuffed the pills inside.

It was going on eleven o'clock when he got to Jason's, and the house was dark and the old vehicle the guy drove wasn't anywhere. Reed parked behind a grove of trees and took his gun out of the glove compartment and slipped it in the holder under his jacket and walked over quietly. He had the snack ready for the dog and when it started snuffling around he tossed the meatball over the fence and waited. Within thirty minutes, the mangy animal lay down and fell asleep, and Reed climbed over the gate. He was in!

First of all, he wanted to check the house as he knew from before the man camped in two rooms, so he very quietly peered again through a tear in a shade in the living room window. The room looked the same, with clothes strewn all over, take-out food cartons sitting on table tops, and this time Jason Edwards was asleep on the bedroll.

Goddammit, Reed muttered. He stepped back realizing the guy must have been hiding the vehicle somewhere all along. Well hell, now that he had come so far, and the watchdog was sound asleep too, he was going to take a look around the place. Mainly the barn! He felt for his gun and darted to the shadows. He crept quietly around the side of the barn and saw it had three entrances, with tire tracks going up to one. Well goddammit, he swore again, so this is where he's been spending his time. But why?

One of the entrances to the inside was partly hidden from the house by a couple of bushes and he ran over and it took barely minutes until he had the door open with one of his specialty tools. He drew his gun, and the minute he stepped in he was enveloped with warmth, humidity and bright lights. When his eyes adjusted he saw rows of potted plants at least three to four feet high. It didn't take Reed long to figure just why Jason Edwards didn't want to be involved in the insurance litigation. For Christ's sake the guy had thousands of dollars tied up in a marijuana crop and he needed to keep a low profile.

Well, fucker, Reed mumbled, you're going to be in the bright lights now! And he took out his cell and called Sheriff Harding. Fifteen minutes later Reed opened the barbed wire gate as a line of official cars came in.

He directed them toward the barn where the illegal weed crop was growing right under their noses. And right then he heard the first shot!

-32-

Inga Mueller had been twenty-one years old when she left the farm and ventured into the big city of Billings, Montana to earn her living. She had taken a course in typing through a mail order house and had been hired by a chain of grocery stores. She had been there for years when her life changed dramatically after getting that call from back home about an accident. Her own life had just started to pick up, since meeting a nice young man in her company. But after the funerals of her sister and husband, when Inga brought their daughter home to raise, sadly the boyfriend wasn't interested in her anymore when he found out he would have to support two people. Inga was heartbroken. There had been a small amount of insurance money, but that had only lasted for a few years. Later Inga was terminated from her job and that's when she had to go to work as a waitress. Things went downhill for the two after that, and Inga blamed Alicia for her problems and was always reminding her that before she came, her life was good. She began leaving the growing young girl at home by herself with orders not to go outside or leave the house for any reason after school. Usually all there was in the house for Alicia to eat was canned soup, no crackers and never cookies or treats of any kind. She grew up lonely knowing she wasn't wanted and was envious of other girls her age having two parents that loved them and wore pretty clothes. She came to hate her aunt, and as soon as she graduated, she left.

Grown up, Alicia was a bleached blonde, with brown eyes, a slim figure and an ample bust-line. She spent a few years around Billings working in bars, and that's when she met Clark who introduced her to the life of a road hustler as they were sometimes called. And now where she had made a niche for herself!

Inga hadn't done too well by herself. All those years of having her sister's kid under foot she'd had to work her fingers to the bone. Doggone, before her sister had gotten herself and her husband killed in that accident her life was great. She'd had a good paying job, a nice orderly house, and a chance for marriage. Then this youngster was thrown in her midst and Inga was unable to adjust. She didn't know how or take time to learn how to help this youngster through her loneliness, or even think of learning to love her as her own child. Instead, Inga let her animosity over it all get the best of her. She didn't love the girl, didn't even like her. She looked just like her mother. Inga was only too happy to see Alicia pack her meager bags and leave. Now she was finally rid of this noose around her neck.

Inga was in her sixties when she started having problems with her memory. She had lived alone now for a few years and would forget to pay her bills or to take her medicine. And Alicia was getting sick and tired of the old bat calling her and whining when her utilities were being threatened because of unpaid bills. And when would she come home? The house needed cleaning and her laundry needed to be done.

"Aunt Inga," Alicia bitched one day, "What the hell do you do all day?"

Inga looked around and shook her head. "What, I just washed the floors yesterday!"

"No, no, you haven't. For God's sake, there's spills and dust all over!" Alicia had a pissed off look on her face.

"But I don't always have time, Alicia. I need to be ready when my boyfriend comes over!"

"Boyfriend," Alicia had gawked at her. "What boyfriend?" She was confounded. "You don't have a boyfriend Inga. It's all in your head," Alicia yelled.

Inga smiled to herself. "Hmm--,"she just mumbled.

Later that day Alicia came back to the house. "Listen to me, Inga. I've arranged for help to come in and cook meals for you and clean. Now I have to get back to my job, but I want you to listen to them. Don't call me!"

Damn, she was tired of the crazy-old bag. So what, Inga had raised her when her folks had died in that accident years ago, was this turnaround? For Christ's sake, she didn't remember even getting a hug from this strait laced old crow.

A few days went by and one morning Inga's helper had called mentioning a man from the neighborhood had been coming over pretty often.

"What, who?" Alicia asked.

"That widower from a couple doors down," the care-giver whispered.

"Is Inga close by the phone now?" Alicia asked outraged. "Let me talk to her!"

And when Inga was handed the phone she gushed, "Alicia I am getting married. Don't you see, he has finally made up his mind after waiting all this time for me until I was free!"

"Inga, forget that old crap!" And Alicia slammed down the phone. Dammit, apparently Inga still thought her old boyfriend from years ago was back. Now she had to take time off, get a car again and go see what the hell that was about.

Hours later, Alicia was back in Billings and she stopped first at another neighbor's house for a cup of coffee where she got an earful. "Listen Alicia," the woman went on, "we've all heard Inga is coming into big money soon now, and this bad ass is after it! He's tried it before with other women.

"How do you know all this?"

"Oh, Inga tells us everything. And we all know he will just marry her and take her money and leave her penniless! But Inga says you know about it and you say it's okay!"

"Oh, for God's sake," Alicia mumbled on her way back to the house. After all the work I've done getting this case set up where I'll finally have millions, this fucker thinks he's going to get rich! I don't think so--, she had raged as she got near the house. And just then as the neighbor had backed his vehicle down her driveway, Alicia had reached under the seat in her rented car for her .38 aimed and blew him away.

Several hours later Alicia had just gotten back to the house after a few stiff belts of whiskey in a downtown Billings bar as Inga had called on her cell and wailed, "He's gone, now what will I tell my girlfriends. I was going to get married today!"

"Well, tell them you discovered he's a bum only out to steal your money!" Alicia had exclaimed out of patience.

-33-

Lindy Lewis took a chaise lounge chair out to the beach by the water and stretched out. Her fair Scandinavian skin was golden as she slathered herself with oil and then lay back and closed her eyes. She'd had some coffee and toast for breakfast and wanted to relax this morning before she put her sign out front declaring she was home and available for her friends. She'd spent the previous evening with Louie Lui at Shirlee's Place and had a lovely dinner and then spent the rest of the night in his bed. This morning feeling tired and just a little bit hung-over, she felt somewhat irritated with herself for getting into bed again with him. After all, there was no future there! But dammit, why did she want a future anyway with a man, she'd just left Reed! For cripes sake, I don't really want that. I'd have to give up my own life; my own house, my cars, my money! And that stopped her. My money, oh no, I've worked hard for that and I won't share. Well hell, she murmured, I love my life just as it is and I'm not willing to change a thing.

The alarm on her cell phone chirped then after a few hours reminding her it was time to get out of the sun. Back inside, she showered and dressed in a gaily patterned dress of lime green and white, applied her makeup and brushed her blonde hair into a curly cap. After a quick sandwich she put her sign out front declaring she was ready for business. But today for some reason no one came by. It was going on four o'clock and she was ready to close when Shirlee rang her doorbell.

"What on earth is wrong?" Lindy asked her friend seeing her worried face.

"Lindy," Shirlee said coming in hurriedly, now I know where I've seen your friend Louie before!"

"What? Shirlee, you didn't say anything about meeting him before, last night."

"I wasn't sure! Then I remembered seeing him around town here about a year ago."

"It couldn't have been him he said he's never been here before!" Lindy went on, somewhat ticked off at Shirlee's comment.

"I was at a garden party at a friend's house last summer. A lot of people were in and out that afternoon and evening and I swear he was among them!"

"Did you notice who he was with?" Lindy asked.

"Strangers to me, so I called and asked my friend, the hostess of the event, and she said he was with some people who have summer homes here in Hilton Head."

"Really," Lindy exclaimed again digesting that for a moment. Now what the hell was that about? Why would Louie Lui, a builder of up-scale hotels need to cover up his ever being in Hilton Head? And for some reason a chill crept up Lindy's spine.

Shirlee looked around Lindy's lovely living room. "Got a cup of coffee?" She asked.

"Sorry, Shirlee, my mind is in a tailspin. Come in and let's have some wine instead!" Lindy offered, leading the way first to the wine cooler in the kitchen and then with a tray of fixings, out to the lanai facing the ocean.

"Okay my friend, this is more like it!" Shirlee exclaimed sitting down on a soft linen, covered easy chair.

Lindy was busy pouring the wine, and after settling into a matching chair said, "Let's toast our friendship, should we?" And they raised their glasses. And after an afternoon together, Shirlee left to get ready for the evening at her Place and Lindy went back to the lanai, where she sat still ruminating about

Louie's lying about ever being in Hilton Head. What was the reason he would cover that up? But damn, she'd find out!

The days flew by and Lindy was busy with her following. Every afternoon brought a few who needed Lindy's expert advice and every week she made a trip to the bank with a purse full of bills. Lordy, her safe deposit box was bursting so she'd soon have to get another one. She could have deposited all of the bills into one of her accounts, but she liked to have ready cash, just in case. Today she was in a good mood as she left the bank and climbed back into her Mercedes, and as she did a black SUV with two men sat a few cars over and watched her every move. They were right behind her as she stopped by the library for her supply of mystery books, and as she opened her car door to get out a bearded man shoved her over and got in, then the passenger door opened and another smaller man slid in. Now she was held helplessly in between them on the hard console seat and each one had a gun jammed in her ribs.

Lindy sucked in her breath, as one whispered, "Okay hand it over!"

"What?" was all she could say at the moment, their action so smooth.

"Lady don't play dumb with us!" The two men wore hoodies to hide their faces, and sunglasses to cover their eyes.

"Who are you? What the hell do you want?" Lindy whispered, not daring to move.

"We saw you come out of the bank, so hand over the cash or we'll blow you head off!" Now one of the men raised his gun to her head and growled, "Bang, just like that!" Out of the corner of her eye, Lindy noticed he had a snake tattooed on each of his fingers.

It was a hot day and she hadn't had time yet to start the car for the air conditioner to come on, and now as she sat wedged in between the two men she could feel perspiration run down her back. She could also smell them as they reeked of onions and stale liquor.

"We don't have all day, hand the cash over now!" The smaller man growled.

Lordy, her own .38 was just a few feet from her in the glove compartment. If she could only get close enough to get at it. "I don't have any," Lindy tried fiercely to control her shaking voice.

"We'll see, about that." The guy with the beard grabbed her purse and shook it on the floor of the car by their feet. And the envelope with her hundred-dollar bills fell out along with her makeup bag and other articles.

"Looky here what we got." He said holding up a fist full of bills. "Okay, lady we need your wheels!" And in seconds, the one in the passenger side opened the door jumped out, hit her on the side of her head with his gun, then pulled her out and pushed her down to the pavement, and leaving her laying there stunned, while the other man started the Mercedes and they sped off.

There were several cars in the lot by the library and now a man ran over. "Are you hurt?" he asked as Lindy managed to sit up. "Take it easy, here let me help you," and he reached down and took her hand and carefully helped her stand up. One knee was bruised and bleeding and her beautiful dress had ripped in the seam.

"I saw those men take off in the blue Mercedes, what in the world happened?" He had a puzzled look on his face.

"Will you call 911 for me please? Those men just stole my car!" Lindy gasped and leaned against the next vehicle parked in the lot for support.

"I'm on it," he said opening the back door of the vehicle, "this is my car, here you can sit down!" And within ten minutes they heard sirens blaring and then a brown and tan sedan flew into the parking lot.

Now that she didn't have guns jammed in her ribs, Lindy had time to get pissed and she gasped to the Chief of Police, "you've got to find them. Those assholes stole my car, a thousand dollars of my money, my purse with all my identification, and a gun that is in the glove compartment! I do have a license to carry!" She added.

"Slow down please lady. I need your name and address. And what happened here?" Then, seeing her distress, let the witness talk. "I saw it all," the man said. "My name is Tom Hunter and here's the license number of her car.

Chief Joyce was busy writing the report and then looking at Lindy commented, "I have the medics coming and I suggest going with them to the hospital to get checked out."

"No, I'm fine. But I need to catch up with those thieving bastards chief, they've got everything!" Lindy exclaimed raising her voice.

"Relax Miss Lewis I've already got my men on it. They won't get far!"

"I can give the lady a ride home chief if you don't need her for anything more!" Tom Hunter said.

"I'll need Miss Lewis to come in and make a statement first!" The chief commented.

And finally, back at her house, Lindy climbed out of Tom Hunter's car saying, "Thanks for your help, I appreciate your willingness to get involved."

The man smiled, and Lindy saw he was a good-looking man! Lordy, her eyes lit up.

"I saw a lady in distress, I had too!" he remarked. "I have to take off now, but can I call you?"

"Yes!" Lindy answered. Then instead of going in her house and lying down and resting as the sheriff suggested, she opened the garage door and backed another vehicle out. At the time she had bought this fourteen-year-old red convertible from a neighbor who had needed money, she'd just parked it in her garage. Now she was glad she had still kept it. She stepped on the gas and sped out of her neighborhood.

She drove back to the parking lot where everything had just happened, and just in time saw the back of the black SUV, the same vehicle they had been in, just leaving. Lindy punched down on the accelerator and within seconds she was right behind them. Apparently, they had come back for their own vehicle. But where the hell was her Mercedes now?

With one hand she dialed 911 again. When the chief came on the line she said she was following the men who had just robbed her at gun point as she was leaving the bank.

"Miss Lewis stop! You're putting yourself in danger."

"I want my stuff back, and I'm going to stay on them, until you get here!" Lindy had put her on speaker and dropped the cell on to the car seat.

"Where the hell are you now?" The chief asked.

And she gave the closest cross streets adding, "I don't know what they did with my car, but I've got them two cars ahead of me now. It's a black SUV and here's the license number!"

For the next few minutes they were weaving in and out through heavy rush hour traffic in downtown Hilton Head. Lindy didn't know if the chief was on the way or not, and she was getting madder by the minute. Dammit, she cursed!

Then finally she saw the black and white colored vehicle of the police department speeding up to her in her rear-view mirror and she quickly signaled to pull over and got out of the way. And as soon as the chief had the thieves in front, Lindy pulled in behind them and followed. She wouldn't rest until she had her car and purse, and her goddamned thousand bucks back! The chief followed then turning on the flashing lights and siren, but the SUV wouldn't stop and began to speed as it got out to the highway.

Lindy was right behind as their speed increased to eighty, then ninety miles an hour. The air now was freezing in Lindy's vehicle, but she didn't have time to fumble around to turn the AC down as her eyes were glued to the road. She was damned if she was going to stop, and actually it was rather exciting to be in a chase.

Then suddenly she saw the front window on the passenger side in the car explode. OMG! Then apparently a deputy took aim at the tires of the SUV, and in melee of noise and flying dust the vehicle swerved all over the road, then flipped and landed upside down, all this seemed in slow motion, but happened at high speed.

The chief stopped and she and the deputy ran over to the upside-down SUV, guns in hand. They saw the two men pinned under the collapsed dashboard.

In the hullabaloo, Lindy stopped her car with screeching brakes, jumped out and ran over. "Arrest them!" she exclaimed excitedly peering in through a broken window and recognizing the same snake tipped hand of the man who had held that gun pointed at her head only minutes before, lying helplessly now.

"That's them Chief Joyce! Where in the hell is my car and my money?" she yelled at them. She had thrown off her high heeled sandals in her garage and slipped on some flip flops and she stood now in her ripped dress looking rather disheveled.

"Miss Lewis, this is a crime scene, what the hell are you doing here?" The chief yelled. "Step away, I ordered you to go home!"

"Well you did," Lindy exclaimed, "but I needed to go and check out where this had happened to me! And there they were just leaving the place again apparently back to pick up their SUV! I had no choice Chief!"

And then again with still more sirens blaring, more men from the police department rushed the area with their guns drawn, and then a wild shot exploded and Lindy fell to the ground!

-34-

She had just polished the beautiful wood in the kitchen and dining room floors and would set the table next. She had her family coming over this evening for dinner. There would be her sister and girls and then her brother and his large family. Twelve in all and at last she could proudly show off her new house that she and her husband had labored on for a good two years. Now she had room to seat everyone at one big table. Actually, when it wasn't being used it sat four nicely for an intimate dinner. She inhaled softly as a picture of last week when she'd entertained crept back in her thoughts. Her girlfriend and hubby had come over for cocktails and dinner.

Time seemed not to matter to Lindy as sometimes the scenes were delightful and other times somewhat baffling. Like now why was someone continually calling her name and gently slapping her cheek? Everyone knew her name. "Leave me alone," Lindy mumbled turning away from the irritating intrusion.

And then she was able to resume the things she had to get done in time for her party. Her husband came in then from the garage carrying the bottles of wine he'd just purchased at the liquor store and put several to chill in the wine refrigerator and opened and set the reds on the kitchen counter to breath. Lindy smiled at him and said "Thanks sweetie," and blew him a kiss. He swatted her on the butt as he hurried by, "How long are you going to starve me until I can eat something?" he asked with a sad look on his face, but behind a smile. The guy loved her cooking and was always hungry.

Delicious aromas surrounded the kitchen from the standing rib roast with garlic cloves baking in the oven. How she loved her new kitchen with the expensive stainless steel, gas burner stove she had always wanted. Opening the doors on the wooden cupboards for the serving dishes, and the dinner plates from their own standing shelves she carefully set the table. It seemed another lifetime since she had lived in that old townhouse that they had bought when they had first gotten married. Even then she had had plans of finding her dream home.

And it was several years later when she had found it. A rundown old mansion that had been left standing forlornly almost hidden in among tall trees, bushes and weeds. They discovered it one day out on a drive down through some dirt roads on the outskirts of Minneapolis. The minute Lindy had set eyes on it she knew somehow it was going to be hers!

"Stop, stop the car sweetie," Lindy remembered exclaiming to her husband.

"At that old rundown place, it's a wreck!" He had said. But slowed the car and she was climbing out even before he had come to a stop.

They had walked around it, then stepped carefully up on the three-sided deck over the rotting boards and peeked in the windows.

"Do you see that two-sided fireplace?" She said wiping a cleaner spot on the glass. "See it must burn on both sides, in the kitchen and what could be the living room!" Lindy exclaimed excitedly.

"This place is old and looks like it needs to be torn down Lindy!" He had said.

Her heart sank at his comment. "Oh no, sweetie don't you see. We could bring this back to its original beauty!"

"Maybe we could, but it would take a long time and use up all our savings. Would you be willing to commit to working that hard?" He asked.

"Lordy, it's just what I've been waiting for!" And then they had found a spot under a fruit tree of some kind and sat down and just looked at the place. They found out that week the original owners had been killed in an accident decades ago and distant relatives kept up the taxes and were glad to get it off their hands so they bought it!

Then Lindy and her husband had begun the renovation on the outside first with new windows, siding and shingles and paint. Then had the short gravel road and driveway graded and tarred for easy access. And, finally they were ready to start on the inside. There they cleaned out bird nests, bee hives and mice nests and had all the wild life ousted. To their wonderful surprise, they found out the floors were all oak and just needed sanding as well as the inside doors and baseboards. All the cupboards went, but they were able to save the walls with the crown mold ceilings. In the master bedroom the most glorious large crystal chandelier still hung safely covered in a plastic bag which Lindy had carefully taken down and spent days cleaning. She felt the shine of it in her eyes now.

Then someone slipped something smelling just horrible under her nose and instead of the enjoyable cooking aromas from the roasting dinner in her kitchen, it took her breath away and made her gasp. She took several deep breaths, and then the all-white room edged its way through her foggy thoughts. Lindy opened her eyes to strangers who all stood peering down at her curiously.

"Miss Lewis welcome back." And a man in a white coat held out his hand and said, "Can you tell me how many fingers you see?"

"Ah---, for cripes sake, five!" Lindy remarked grogginess slurring her words.

"And what year is this?" He went on.

"It was 2017 last I 'member," Lindy answered. Then she became aware of a hot burning pain in her shoulder and groaned.

"You were lucky Miss Lewis the bullet that got you could have been much worse and hit a vital area. But it did major damage to your shoulder muscle. I just gave you a shot intravenously so in a minute you'll feel better! And although tests show you should be okay, I'd like to keep you here for a few days."

Lindy lay still and let the medicine take hold and soon she was back to her happy place of drug induced daydreams.

-35-

Something was irritating Jason Edwards's dream tonight as he lay tumbled in his bedroll made up of an old quilt on an older mattress he'd found in the junk in the house he had taken over as his temporary home at the abandoned farm on the outskirts in Billings Montana.

"Fucking mosquitoes," he mumbled swatting feebly in his sleep. He'd had a few more beers than usual tonight and had fallen into a drunken stupor. But something else awakened him now. He realized it was that goddamned mangy dog he'd found hanging around the countryside and had brought here to be a guard dog, snuffling outside by the barn. Then all was quiet and he turned over and fell back into his slumber, but one thing he had was very good hearing, and suddenly he heard someone or something brushing up against the side of the house. He jumped up awake now and grabbed the gun that he always kept right next to him by his bedroll. When he peeked through a tear in the shade covered window, he caught the back of a man running, bent low, over to the barn. That's the fucker who was here before asking questions about that goddamned accident. Why in hell was he sniffing around the barn? He watched, then the intruder disappeared and Edwards thought, maybe the fucker has gotten tired of nosing around and given up and left. Then a flash of light suddenly flared from inside the barn.

Jason Edwards stood paralyzed! The fucker had gotten inside! And he saw his dream of stacks of greenbacks crumbling. He stepped quietly outside in his dirty cut offs but couldn't see where the man had gone. He crept around the old buildings to get a better look and then he found the dog but couldn't tell if it was sleeping or dead! And that really pissed Edwards off. Did the guy shoot a harmless animal?

All was quiet and maybe ten minutes went by as Edwards quietly crept around the buildings searching for the intruder. He saw the trespasser as he stood now just inside a door he had opened into the barn. Edwards took aim and shot at the low down nosy interloper. He hated that fucker. In the darkness he couldn't tell if the man went down or had taken cover.

And then he saw the line of sheriff's vehicles come in his driveway and he knew it was too late!

Jesus H. Christ! Having no time, he took off running like hell into the woods that spread around the old farm. The state had voted years ago that the trees be left as part of the forest that they connected with. It was miles and miles of trees, caves and hills and places you could hide in.

And Jason Edwards knew the area well as he always had a plan B in mind. If someone tried to follow his tracks through the weeds it would eventually lead them right back to the farm. He was a cunning man who had grown up on the streets and didn't have an ounce of respect for any individual who represented the law. Now his dream was going up in smoke, but the assholes would not get him. No-siree! I've had my other wheels stashed in the woods, Edwards mumbled. He was pissed and deadly.

It took him about ten minutes to find his way in the forest and then to his SUV and soon he was on the road away from his crop that was almost ready to harvest. Bastards, I only needed a few more days! Now he wondered how many do-gooders would get their hands on the weed and save a bag for themselves before turning it all over to the cops. And really who was this asshole that was asking questions about that traffic accident. Conners or Cooper was his name, Edwards mumbled. Could he be a dirty SOB from ATF who was keeping the information of the place for himself, and maybe the local cop? Edward's ten-year-old SUV was blue with cussing as he flew out of city and on to the freeway to get far away from the hills of Montana.

He didn't know exactly where in the hell to go, but he guessed it would be the smartest to head north away from any big cities. He had a buddy who owned a spot in the woods near a lake way up north or if he just kept on going he could end up in Canada. All you needed to do then was get over a fence. So, he settled in for the ride, but before he got close he stopped at a gas station and changed his clothes, cut off his long hair and put on a pair of glasses. He thought about shaving his head but couldn't take the time to do that. Maybe later. Years ago, he'd spent days erasing his fingers of their prints. A trick he'd learned one time while he spent some time behind bars from an old buzzard that had been caught red handed while having a heart attack during one of his many hoists.

"Here's what you do, little buddy," the old thief confided. "Go buy a pineapple, a nice ripe one. Then you cut it up and eat the innards!" The old fart had laughed then at himself. "But now here comes the good part. You take the peelings and rub them on your hands and your fingers every day. You buy more as you run out and do this every day for a good month and I guarantee you will not have any prints left for them to identify you with."

Yup, you goddamn fuckers, he consoled himself as he drove, totally pissed at losing his fortune, just try to find me! And already he was thinking of his next plan, but first of all he needed money! Then a shot tore into a front tire of his vehicle and it turned over and rolled. By a miracle he was unhurt.

-36-

Lindy Lewis lay covered up to her chin in a hospital room in Hilton Head, SC. After midnight she could get another shot of morphine for the pain after the surgery in her shoulder if needed. As yet the hospital office following the protocol of locating someone to take over the responsibility of a patient, and nothing had been found of any report of a missing woman. And without any of her identification all they knew was her slurred murmuring of Lindy Lewis which didn't tell them much. The sheriff hadn't gotten back to them yet with any more information he had, as he had to rush out to take care of a crisis, so she was known as the mysterious patient in room 101. At around 1:00 a.m., when a night nurse checked on her she found the patient seemed distressed in her breathing and she quickly took her blood pressure and heart rate, then sounded the alarm for help and the crash cart!

In minutes the room was overcrowded with hospital attendants, all intent on their own duties. Her covers were thrown off and a mask was clamped over her face for oxygen. Drugs were hastily injected into the IV that ran into her wrist.

In her foggy distraught state Lindy worried, Oh Lordy what was going on? She laid stock still as the hospital staff waited and watched the monitor. She was cold and felt her gown was missing, but she didn't mind, why did they make you wear such worn, shapeless rags anyway? She felt the cooler air hit her body as her numbers bounced out of the monitor while the staff stood watching. Lindy lay still, naked at this point so everyone could watch for any signs of seizure.

And then finally she was out of the crisis and was covered up with warmed blankets and the rosy pain-free feeling spread over her body again. She had instinctively felt the room empty of strangers who had rushed in and out. And now thankfully she fell back into the drugged imagery of years past.

Today she was cooking a zesty beef stew and dumplings for dinner and she was waiting for her husband's call to let her know he was through at the doctor's office for his annual check-up and on his way home.

Finally, the phone rang and when Lindy answered, she heard him say in a strangled voice, "Lindy, they just told me I have cancer. I've got lung cancer!"

"What?" she managed to whisper. Then she sat down on a stool at the kitchen counter as her legs buckled.

"I've just had a c-scan and it is a silver dollar sized spot."

Then she asked, "Are they sure?"

"Yes, but they say to get another opinion." His voice was hoarse.

"Lordy," she murmured, tearfully catching her breath.

Lindy sucked in her breath and didn't want to start crying. "Listen sweetie," she managed, "hurry home and we'll talk about it!" She turned off the stew simmering on the stove and sat down as it seemed her world started a downward spiral.

Time slid by in Lindy's dreams but suddenly she shivered in the warm bed as she was attacked by black ants, hundreds of them crawling all over her body.

She screamed and alarmed a nurse in training who was straightening her bed covers who ran for help. Then in her dream, Lindy felt relief from the predators as flames reached skyward burning them. She sighed in her slumber and was silent again.

The next day, the Hilton Head sheriff stopped in to check on Lindy Lewis, the victim who had been robbed at gunpoint and then shot. He brought her identification with him as it had been found on the floor of the Mercedes when they had located it.

"Her address is in Minnesota," he commented to a nurse in charge. "Is she awake yet?" he asked.

"Yes, she's awake this morning and giving us hell," the nurse answered dryly.

And they walked into Lindy's room to find her sitting on the edge of her bed. And as soon as she saw the sheriff, she straightened, "Did you find those assholes who stole my car, my money and my purse?" She took a step to meet him but realized she was tethered to the IV running in to her wrist.

"Careful!" The nurse went running over to Lindy. "You don't want to rip this IV out miss."

Lindy grabbed at the cord and steadied herself.

"Yup, we've got the thieves locked up and they'll face charges. They admitted they've been watching you!" The sheriff commented.

"I hope they rot in hell! Did you get my stuff back?" she asked.

"I have your wallet here, Miss Lewis." Then nodding to the nurse asked, "When will she be discharged?"

"I'm not sure but the doctor will be in soon again to check on her."

"Where is the thousand dollars that I had in my purse? My money?" Lindy wanted to know.

"Everything we found on them except your wallet here is in an evidence box down at the station. It's all part of a crime scene for now, but you can get it back soon, after coming down to the station to identify what's yours."

"Well, I had just been to my bank and withdrew a thousand dollars from my account. Did you get it all back?" Lindy demanded, never wanting to be far from her money. Sitting in her bed in a faded hospital gown that fell off one shoulder, her hair in a mess and her face devoid of make-up, she looked every bit her age. Lindy sank back exhausted on the bed after her outburst. She was soon dozing again feeling the effects of the drugs that relieved the bitching pain.

-37-

Inga Mueller sat in the back seat of the sheriff's car like an obedient child. Why didn't the man have the decency to take these awful bracelets of my wrists before I had to get in here? She whispered to herself. Now she sat perched precariously on the edge of the seat as they careened around corners and curves on their way to his "downtown offices", he had declared when they'd left her house.

Now what in the world did he mean when he said 'he was taking me in?' Inga's mixed up reasoning stumped her again.

Wasn't she supposed to see her boyfriend this morning when he came over to pick her up? And weren't they going to Vegas to get married today? She impatiently knocked on the glass partition that separated the front and back seats in the vehicle.

"Mr. Police Man," she said, "we need to hurry and get this done, I've got to get ready as I'm to leave for a trip this morning!" Inga ran a hand over her messy hair and smoothed her dress. She was wearing a blue paisley print that came down over her knees and flip flops on her feet.

"Well you won't be going anywhere today except down to my office." The sheriff checked her in his rear-view mirror as he talked. "I need to take a statement and get your prints."

"Then we must hurry so I don't have to make him wait!" Inga said with anxiety in her voice.

"Mrs. Mueller, don't you remember your boyfriend won't be coming over?" He asked patiently.

"No, no I don't! Alicia said he was shot, but sometimes she's mean to me." Inga looked around guiltily and then nervously at her surroundings, as if seeing them for the first time.

"Mrs. Mueller, what she was telling you is that your boyfriend is dead. Someone shot him!" He watched for her reaction.

"Oh no," Inga cried, "Who would do that?" She caught his inquiring face in the rearview mirror. "He is a nice man and I'm going to marry him!"

Oh Lord, he needed to get the doc down there to run some tests. This poor woman needed help, and he couldn't do a thing until he got a medical report of her condition.

Down at his office he helped her out of his vehicle, and then called for his female officer who was on duty to come give him a hand.

"Deputy June will help you now to a room where you can lie down and rest, Mrs. Mueller, and I'll come and see you soon," he said to Inga. She wasn't sure if she should thank him or not.

Back in his office he put in a call to the medical department and left a message for the doctor to come over and check out a woman whom he had brought in for questioning.

It was early afternoon when the sheriff arrived back at the murder scene at Inga Mueller's house. The lot was roped off with the yellow "crime scene" tape and two deputies were guarding the area surrounding the house.

"Sheriff Harding," Reed Conners said, "We didn't get much of a chance to talk when we met the other day, when you arrested my client, Jason Edwards. I'm an attorney and an investigator with the Federated Insurance Company located in Minneapolis, Minnesota."

"Mr. Conners, what can I do for you here?"

Reed swiped a hand through his hair on his forehead. "I'm looking into an accident report filed by Inga Mueller. She was hurt while driving her car a number of weeks ago. And the report claims my client is guilty."

"You're saying your client injured Inga Mueller. She was driving a car?" The sheriff looked at Reed and shook his head.

"Yup. Happened a while back." Reed said.

"And your driver was the pot growing individual we just picked up and arrested today?"

"One and the same sheriff," Reed commented.

"Jesus H. Christ, so I got them both sitting in my cells!" He puffed out a breath.

"Looks that way," Reed Conners almost laughed.

"Son of a bitch!" the sheriff swore.

"Your boys just caught me up on what's gone on here so far. You took this Inga Mueller in for murder now?" Reed asked.

"Naw, she's got Alzheimer or something, ---too far gone. I had to get her out of here so we could investigate."

"Do you mind if I hang around for a while?" Reed asked.

"No, glad to have you aboard Conners, this whole thing is turning into what is called a "cluster fuck"! The sheriff of Billings said.

"Have you met her niece Alicia Mueller yet?" Reed asked,

"Just a while ago. Now there's a piece of work!"

"Well sheriff, it's a weird situation. I don't know what to believe yet, but I have a notion the niece

Alicia is behind this! Alicia is a liar, the plaintiff Inga is helpless, and my client Jason Edwards has a laundry list of arrests already and now for growing an illegal substance! Has the gun been found yet that killed the man?" Reed asked.

Just then the sheriff's cell rang. He listened intently to the info as it was rattled off. And clicking off he said, "The victim was identified as Maynard Fielding, he was a retired National Guard officer and he was 68 years old. Looks like the bullet may have come from a .45."

"Was his address listed as right here next door?" Reed asked,

"That's what they said."

Just then the door opened and Alicia Mueller stepped out. "Where in the hell is my dear aunt?" She asked, putting her hands on her hips.

"Like I told you before, I needed to take her in for questioning so she's down at my headquarters!"

She scowled at them both while standing on the porch. "Are you planning on arresting her for killing that man?" She asked.

Sheriff Harding looked at her and said, "Hmm--, not as yet. I've got some other ideas I need to check out."

"I'm going to lock up the house now as I've got to get back to my job." Alicia Mueller remarked as she stood dressed in jeans and boots, with a jean jacket thrown on over a t-shirt. Her blonde hair was still wet and brushed back off her face.

"Miss Mueller, you have to leave the house open as its now part of a crime scene! By the way, does Inga have any other family around here?" Harding asked.

"Nope, I'm it," Alicia said. "See that your guys don't totally destroy this place, you've got my cell number so you can call me," She said. And she stepped away from the house carrying her shoulder bag and walked with a sway in her hips to her rental car that stood parked on the street.

Both men stood there and watched, and then Reed said to the Sheriff of Billings, "My friend, that woman has the answers to this whole mess."

"Yup, and I also know just where to find her when I'm ready!"

"Me too," Reed Conners commented dryly but laughed. "Let me know and we'll go together and shower her with dollar bills!"

-38-

Lindy Lewis had lain in a fog partly from the drugs they had given her for the pain caused by the path the bullet had made through her shoulder, and from the surgery itself. Now as she lay in the hospital bed in Hilton Head savoring the effects of the drugs, she wondered if she should call one of her brothers in the north and ask them to come down and stay with her. She had always been able to take care of herself and she had managed to get herself out of many predicaments but suddenly here she was; hurting, lonely and feeling downtrodden by what had happened to her. Tears ran down her cheeks and wet the pillow in her sorrow. All her friends, her lovely home and her business were forgotten and she was back to being a young girl herding cattle on faraway meadows on the ranch.

She remembered carrying her food for the day in a paper bag, and a long stick for tapping disobedient baby calves when they tried to run away from the group. She wondered why she was always chosen for this job! Was she a troublemaker in her large family and her folks sent her away for some peace? But oh, the loneliness of being out there all by herself. She sighed in her sorrow then a faint smile crossed her face as she remembered. But here's where she learned to twirl that stick and become a majorette later in her high school marching band. And here's where she learned to yodel. In her home the radio was only played when her dad allowed it, and singers by the name of Brenda Lee, Patsy Cline and others brought stars to her eyes. Out here in the meadows, miles away from anyone, she could sing her songs and yodel like the best of them while twirling her stick. Hours would go by and when the sun started to go down that's when twelve-year-old Lindy would round up her herd and start for home. At least a couple times a week she was told to take the herd to another pasture to graze on the alfalfa. And on days when the winds were gentle her songs could be heard spreading over the countryside. Lindy drifted for some time, unaware if it was days or hours. Then something woke her, brought her to the surface of reality. She opened her eyes and gazed around at the strange room.

"Where in the hell am I?" she yelled loudly. When no one showed up to check the noise, she sat up in the bed but almost toppled out of it. Lindy had been drugged but now the time and place began to right itself in her head. And after being taken off the pain killer, a day later she was ready to go home.

How happy she was to be there again in her home on the shore of the great ocean. She began to exercise and walk the beach again and within days her shoulder wound had healed nicely and she was back to her old self. She put her sign out for her friends to see and soon she was sought after for her readings and physic predictions and her days were filled. There were troubled romances, a lost teen, a prayer for health and an old woman who wanted to die and be with her husband. Lindy's coffers began to bulge again with money. She was feeling good but now kept her gun close.

One thing though that niggled in her mind was the statement her friend Louie Lui from Minneapolis had made when he'd been in town a while back, he had said that he had not been to Hilton Head before. It was strange! Why would he lie about never being there before? And Lindy believed her friend Shirlee when she told her that she had seen him at a friend's party about a year ago. Later that morning she called Shirlee.

"Let's get together for lunch one day soon," Lindy said.

"Okay, I'd love that. Will tomorrow work for you?" Shirlee asked, "I'm taking a week off and closing my place to get some updating done in there."

"Really," Lindy said, "what are you doing?"

"I'm putting in a new sound system and getting our outside area redone. So, I'm free tomorrow." Shirlee commented.

"I'll come by and pick you up at eleven o'clock, if that's okay?" Lindy exclaimed.

"That sounds good to me. See you then."

Later the next day, over coffee and a lovely dessert, Lindy asked the question that had been burning in her mind. "Shirlee, do you know who Louie Lui was with here in town, when you saw him at your friend's party last year?"

"Yes, I do. He was with a group of people who have vacation homes here. I found out from my friend it was the D'Agustino's."

Lindy suddenly felt sick and took a calming breath as a chill crawled down her back. "Oh my God," she whispered, "did you say D'Agustino?"

"Why?" Shirley asked.

"Because my friend, don't you remember the scandal several years ago when I had dated Mario D'Agustino and witnessed a murder?"

"Yes, now I do, although it was not widespread here in vacation land. You see the papers here downplay anything about our residents. But listen to this it reminds me that I heard someone in that family owns the paper here in town."

"Well, no wonder. If you have time I can refresh your memory and tell you the real story!" Lindy commented dryly and they ordered another glass of wine.

"You mean to say that two men from that family were killed up there in your guy's hometown?" Shirlee asked awestruck.

"Yes," Lindy took a breath. "You see I had to testify for the FBI against the one I dated and he was found not guilty. But later he and his brother showed up to make me pay. It all resulted in Mario and his brother, two D'Agustino men getting killed in Birch Lake!"

"Really," Shirlee repeated.

Awhile back I found out the family has second homes here on the island. At first, I wanted to run, then I decided to stay and live my life here on this island, but now I'm worried what this is all about."

"Did you get to know the family?" Shirlee asked.

"Just the brother Andre. Years ago, when I first came here a friend of mine visited me and we met Mario and Andre. They said they were in town with a shipload of merchandise. Of course, we didn't know they were drug lords and that's what they were bringing in. They charmed the heck out of us and we believed their story. But after a few weeks the whole affair exploded when I was out on the ocean with

Mario and I saw him kill a man and toss his body overboard!"

"Oh my God," Shirlee whispered. "I've been invited to a party a few times over on their side of the island, but I've never gone. Between you and me, I never felt safe around them! And they come into my place quite often!"

"I guess all you can do is keep your distance," Lindy commented. "But now I know that Louie is a friend of that family. I remember there were several nephews and they must have stepped up and taken over the reins, but I'm sure it is all still controlled by the ancient Mama D'Agustino.

"Small world," Shirlee murmured.

"But here's a thought my good friend," Lindy commented as a chill ran down her back. "It leads me to wonder if the D'Agustino drug money has financed Louie Lui's hotel right here in the states, the new one in Minneapolis. And she went on, "If so he probably knows who I really am and that I was the one who blew the whistle on his friends!"

-39-

Sheriff Harding called Reed Conners to meet him at his office. The report of Inga Mueller's health had come back from the doctor. Thirty minutes later Reed was there.

"The doc reports she's well into the throes of Alzheimer's Disease," he said to Reed. "And that he has placed her under care in a nursing home since she does not have any one who can give her full-time care. I find she is not stable enough to withstand a court date to fight the charge of driving that car in the accident report. And here's an aside; the doctor says here he just does not believe she would have been able to drive the car that was involved in that accident in the state of mental health she presents."

"And the man is right!" Reed commented slapping a hand on the sheriff's desk. "But the niece claims her aunt was behind the wheel and this condition of her aunts was caused by the mental strain of the accident! She's saying it caused her to lose her mind and she's suing for five million dollars."

"I got no eye witness of that man's murder either," the sheriff groaned. "However, we found another neighbor of hers, this time from across the street, he had been out watering his garden when he hears this boom, as he called it. When he turned the water off and come around to the front he saw a light-colored sedan car just turning the corner. Then when he looked over to the Mueller house he could see a person slouched over in his vehicle and he called it in."

"Did he know the victim?" Reed asked.

"Nope," the sheriff answered. "Although other neighbors hinted he was romancing the woman of the house."

"What the hell?" Reed swiped a hand through his hair.

"After canvasing the neighborhood we've found its mostly retired seniors who live there and won't contribute much, although they all have their own opinions and like to gossip! So, what do we have so far?" Reed asked.

"Jesus," Sheriff Harding groaned again, "I've got two cases going here; a murder and a car accident.

Well, we do know the murdered victim's identity! And that he was shot to death and found in Inga Mueller's driveway and that a light-colored car was seen leaving the neighborhood. Then we have this accident that car driver Inga was in and she claims she was hit by this man who was drunk. But both the doctor and the neighbor say Inga could not have been driving the car that was involved in the accident with Edwards." He said shaking his head.

"How about I go and visit Inga Mueller. Is she in a nursing home now?"

"Yup, and I'd like your take on her too Reed if you don't mind."

The afternoon was getting hot this fall day in Montana as Reed got directions to the Grace Lutheran Home and the minute he stepped in to the place he could smell the delicious aroma of roasting chicken and bread baking.

"I'd like to see Inga Mueller," he asked a nurse at a reception desk.

"Oh yes, I can bring you to her room." She smiled at him.

Reed followed her through a large gathering room that held a piano and a television, and where some patients looked at him with hope in their eye, then down a hallway where she knocked on a closed door.

"Hello Inga, you've got company."

"Go away, I don't want any," a muffled voice complained.

"It's a handsome man!" She went on to say.

Silence, then Inga said, "My handsome man is dead they say, and now I'm put in here in jail with these crazy people because they think I killed him!"

"Inga, remember me, Reed Conners?" He asked. "Listen to me I don't think you killed your friend!" He could hear her sniffling.

"You don't?" She asked.

"No, and I would like to help you if you'll let me. Just come out." And after a few minutes Inga did.

Now when Reed saw her, after just a few days the poor woman seemed to have shriveled into a little old lady without the spark he had seen before. Her hair was wispy and sticking to her head. And the wrinkles on her face seemed to have deepened. Of course, now she wore no make-up and had been in jail and now here without anyone to help her with her appearance. She ran a hand over her hair and adjusted her jeans and shirt as she looked him over as he stood in her doorway.

"Oh right, now I remember you, you're from that insurance company!" She exclaimed.

"Yes, I am. And Inga," he said, "what are you planning on doing after you get the five million dollars from it?"

"What?" Inga stammered. "What in the world?" She looked at Reed in confusion, not knowing if he was joking or what.

"Oh--, I don't know anything about that!" Inga commented.

Reed patiently studied her. "Listen to me, Inga do you remember driving your car that night when you went to the store? It was late and dark. And when you were making a left turn this pickup ran right into you smashing your car and hurting you?"

Inga looked at him inquiringly as she groped for remembrance. And at TIMES LIKE THIS she just swallowed the fear she had inside. Alicia must be right that she was driving the car that night and she was just too damn old to remember. "But I--," And she put her head down between her hands as a sob shook her small frame.

Reed put a hand on her shoulder and led her over to a chair in her room. As he looked around he was shocked when he saw her room consisted of a curtain divider with a twin bed, a small three-drawer dresser, a small bedside table and one chair. He swore under his breath and kneeled down by her side as she sat in the only chair.

No wonder the poor woman was in shock after seeing what was going to be her home from now on.

"Inga listen to me now, were you behind the wheel of your car when that accident happened?"

She was quiet for some time, then sat up and wiped her eyes on her hands and said, "No, I don't care what Alicia says, I was not!"

Reed touched her shoulder again. "Okay, that's what I thought. Now Inga just lay down on this bed and try to sleep. Things will get better, I promise." And he helped her lie down and put a blanket over her. As he watched she sighed and closed her eyes. Goddamn it, now he was pissed and he hurried out of there. Now where the hell was that niece of hers?

He went out to the farm next where Jason had been living and found his other vehicle, a silver pickup, hidden in an old rundown granary off to the side in the woods on the property. He carefully searched the front of it for signs of a collision, and sure enough he found scrapes and a dent on the front bumper. After patiently wiping it down with a clean white towel it came away with tiny pieces of blue paint. The same color as Inga's old model Buick that sat all banged up in her yard.

Next, he went down to the jail and found Jason Edwards sitting in his cell. "Okay buddy, do you want to come clean about hitting that car the other night?"

"Nah, you figure it out!" Edwards laughed.

Reed Conners walked closer to the cell. "Listen you smart ass punk, you're going to prison for a good fifteen to twenty years for illegally growing cannabis with the intent to market. And with your record you won't be seeing daylight for a long, long time!"

Edward's unshaven face whitened and he mumbled, "Aw- shit!"

"Are you ready for that?" Reed asked pointing a finger at him.

"I want to see a lawyer," Edwards whined.

Reed left and went to see Sheriff Harding, "I got an update. I just saw Inga Mueller at the rest home she's staying at, and she insists she was not driving the car when that accident took place. So that leaves the niece, Alicia. And I got definite evidence that Jason Edwards was driving his vehicle, a pickup that's hidden in an old shack on the property he's been living at.

Sheriff Harding stood up from his file covered desk. "Jesus thanks Conners!" He went over and grabbed his Western hat. "Come on, let's go see the prosecutor with all this and get a court date set." And it was set for the end of the week.

It was getting late in the evening and Reed went back to his hotel and to the bar and ordered a Crown Royal on ice and a steak.

"Should I set you up a table?" Julie, the same good-looking bartender from the other night asked as she leaned over the bar.

"Thanks, I'll eat right here with the scenery," he said enjoying her plunging neckline.

-40-

Lindy started an early walk on the familiar beach which today was crowded with tourists out with their plastic bags scouting for sea shells and other morsels of interest. If you were patient and had a good eye, you might find things like shark's teeth, gun shells hidden in the sand from when the German's invaded the Atlantic shores in World War II, or even pieces of gold that had been said to wash up in the sand. Years ago, when she had first come to Hilton Head Island she scouted the sands too, but finally had enough of the search and enough shells to fill a basket to use as a doorstop.

Today she had a bikini on under a terry cover and a straw hat to keep the sun off her hair with the new shade of blonde she'd had put in. An old Western song called, "Send Me a Bouquet of Roses," was still running through her thoughts after hearing it on television the night before in an old movie. Lordy, she remembered that song way back when she had been a young teenage girl and her mother had taught her how to play a guitar to accompany herself as she sang songs. How she would belt out a number when she babysat the younger kids, after shooing them outside to play and she could have the whole house to herself. She hummed the song as she walked swinging her arms to a beat.

Today she finally felt good after her hospital stay and she loved her life. Then suddenly, out of the blue someone ran up and grabbed her in a vise-like grip and whispered loudly in her ear over the rushing waves from the ocean. "Okay lady, come along or you're dead!"

"What?" Lindy managed to mumble. Then felt something press against her side through the terry cover she wore. "Oh Lord, not again," she thought sickened.

"We've been watching you. Don't waste my time or yours by trying to yell for help, the minute you open your mouth I will pull the trigger on this shooter and you will be scattered all over this pretty sand!"

Lindy stood stock still weighing the situation. She had her gun but she was helpless, as it was on her right side and he had her shoulder and arm pinned down.

She could see it was a man wearing dark glasses with a cap covering his hair. He had on shorts and a loose jacket and had his left hand holding the gun under his jacket poking her in her ribs. He was tall and felt muscular.

"Who the hell are you?" Lindy gasped. "And what do you want from me?" Her throat felt like it was closing up.

"You don't get to ask the questions, but I'll tell you this much, we know you're a snitch, we've been watching you," the man said as he was making her walk with him over dunes and a bridge, and then no doubt toward the woods that covered one side of the island. To other people on the beach it may have looked like they were embracing while they walked, but they couldn't see the fear in her eyes that were hidden under dark glasses.

Lindy's blood ran cold. A snitch, her thoughts were going a mile a minute. Oh Lord, the D'Agustino's! No wonder so many incidences were happening. Apparently, they knew of her and were trying to get rid of her. She had to get away before they got to the woods. He'd kill her. Up ahead she could see the tall trees laden with hanging moss that from a distance looked like ghosts waving their arms beckoning her in. She stopped walking and jerked away from him.

"Hey baby, are you wanting to die right now?" The guy tightened his hold which already felt like a vise around her shoulders.

She obediently walked at his side now, but intentionally took small steps to take up more time. Time to think this out! God, if he got her in the woods, she shivered at the thought of what he might have in mind.

"Listen, I have money. Do you want cash?" She whispered and her voice shook now.

"Nah, I got money. I want you Lindy!"

"Why?" she asked tearfully.

The man laughed in her face. "Because I do!"

"How do you know my name?" Lindy asked.

"We know who you are." He tightened his hold and went on, "And you're mine, and I've patiently waited for this day. By the way, did you ever find my little present I left for you in your refrigerator?"

"And were you one of the assholes that stole my car and my money and then shot me last week?" Lindy gasped.

"Yup, baby! You healed up fast and you're a sexy lil' number and I want to play!" His laughter sounded like cackles.

Lindy swallowed. Oh God, she had to get away from this killer. And right now! She had to take a chance. And she abruptly dropped to a knee and as soon as her left hand touched the sand, she grabbed up a handful of it and tossed it in his face. It all happened in seconds and he suddenly loosened his hold on her. She spun out of his grip and pointed her gun at him.

"Drop it asshole," she screamed, and then again as loud as she could. Luckily a group of teen-age boys, nearby and full of testosterone, slammed him to the ground and his gun went flying through the air. Someone called 911 and soon sirens blared and the beach guards arrived and took over putting handcuffs on the man.

"We're taking him in for questioning Miss Lewis, do you want to press charges?"

"Oh, do I, I've had enough of these clowns. I want to see him behind bars," Lindy exclaimed.

Back at her house, Lindy took a long shower and put on a pot of coffee. Lord, she worried, how long had the D'Agustino family known of her whereabouts?

The next day, Lindy called Shirlee and they met for lunch later in the afternoon at a café called the Bistro of Shelter Cove down on the waterfront. When Lindy looked around the cafe she recognized it was the same place, only renovated, where her and a friend had first met Mario D'Agustino and his brother Andre' several years ago. It had gone from a piano bar to an outside grill with chefs doing their artful cooking and tossing while customers viewed the entertainment involved in cooking their delicious meals. It was a beautiful outside area with red umbrellas over white linen covered tables and red roses in vases topping each. Jazz music flowed softly from the well-known guitarist Dan Thayer as he sat on a stool by the water.

Lindy left her Mercedes with a parking attendant and hurried into the cove mall, her high heels clicking effectively on the concrete pavers. Today she was wearing a black sundress flared at the hemline. And her hair looked just right after she had combed it with her fingers after her shower.

Shirlee came sauntering in wearing a white pantsuit with her brunette hair piled on top her head. They hugged and left their name with the hostess and waited for a table.

"What have you been doing lately?" Shirlee asked as she patted the flyaway wisps of hair over her ears.

Lindy shook her head and laughed, "I picked up another weirdo on the beach who threatened to shoot me!"

"What again? For God's sake Lindy, stay away from there. It's a haven for those praying on tourists and robbing them!" Shirlee whispered.

"Yes, I know. But now I carry my good friend at all times, unfortunately it didn't help me then!" And she opened her purse so Shirlee could see her .38.

"Oh, for God's sake Lindy, someone might see it!" Shirlee gasped. Then their name was called and they were seated at a table in the shade of an umbrella.

After ordering a bottle of Pinot Noir wine they settled in ready to gossip.

"Tell me Shirlee about that new love you mentioned," Lindy smiled.

"You'll never guess who he is," Shirlee said and smiled behind her hand.

"Who?" Lindy asked.

"His name is Rory Calhoun III and he's from New York!"

"Okay, I only remember an old dude by that name from the movie classics on late night television," Lindy commented.

"Well, believe it or not, this is a son of that old actor."

"You're kidding right?" Lindy smiled.

"No, I'm serious. I met him last year as a customer on one of his golfing trips here. And now we've got a long-distance romance going on."

"Wow!" Lindy exclaimed and raised her glass. "We better drink to that, my friend."

And the two women shared a full afternoon of gossip, telling tales and making plans for the next few weeks.

"How is your business going?" Shirlee asked.

"You know it just keeps getting better. Hardly a day goes by where I don't have a number of customers. Only a few show up later in the day, so I'm thinking that I might just open for the mornings from now on.

Shirlee smiled, "Now tell me good friend, really, do you get some superhuman help from somewhere when they ask for help? What do you do?"

Lindy laughed, "Well, I like to hold their hands for a few minutes while looking into their eyes. I encourage them to tell me what they need help with."

"What if they make something up?" Shirlee asked.

"There's that, but then what's the point in coming to see me." Lindy added and laughed.

"Seriously I haven't run across anyone like that yet. And I don't charge for my sessions, although I do accept tips if anyone feels so inclined."

"And they do, don't they?" Shirlee commented. "I know the locals put a high value on the super natural powers so you are definitely on to something!"

"And I almost always get a flash into a person's difficulty and how I might help," Lindy went on.

"Jeepers, I won't be holding hands with you then!" Shirlee laughed.

"Okay," Lindy wiped her lips on the napkin and went on, "Listen I'm thinking of going into Savannah next week to do some shopping and check out some art galleries and probably stay overnight in one of those B and B's I see advertised. Why don't you come along?"

"That just might work, if we can plan it for one of my 'slow nights' at the club." Shirlee said as they raised their glasses in another toast.

-41-

Reed Conners awoke early the next day determined to get a handle on this "cluster fuck," as he thought of the two cases now. He was tired of it all and wanted to get home to Birch Lake as he had too many things left undone at his place. Although he knew his neighbors would be looking after it and call if necessary. But hell, Indian summer as it was called in the Midwest could turn in to the first snowfall of the season anytime now, and he didn't want his boat, which was still sitting in the slip, to get frozen in the water. Now he was sorry he hadn't taken the time and put it in storage before he left.

He showered and dressed and stopped in the coffee shop for a large cup of strong brew on his way into Billings. There was a chill in the air in the mornings and he was wearing a light brown leather jacket today over a white t-shirt and jeans and of course, his western boots. He ran an impatient hand through his hair and brushed it off his forehead.

Goddamn, he had to figure this out now, today! First of all, he had to go see Inga again, and get a sworn statement from her saying she was not driving her car the day of the accident. By God, then he had to find her niece Alicia and get her to admit she was the one behind the wheel of the Buick that night when the pickup hit her as she was making that left turn.

What kind of a person was she to set up her aunt to take the fall? And sure, Inga was mixed up sometimes, but then, at times she was as lucid as anyone else!

This morning when Reed got to the nursing home, Inga was up sitting at a table in the dining room having coffee with a group of ladies. She jumped up when she saw him come in the door and ran over and hugged him.

"This is my friend Reed." She announced happily to them and they all mumbled a greeting.

"Could we talk somewhere in private please?" He asked and she led him over to a quiet corner where they sat down.

"Inga, I need something really important today. And do you mind if I record this? I don't want to forget anything!"

"Oh, I don't mind Reed. Anything you need is fine."

Thank goodness, today Inga was smiling and seemed in her right frame of mind. Reed set his cell phone to record a video and took her picture to go with it. "Okay, remember last time I was here you said that you were not driving your car at the time it was involved in that accident? Can you definitely acknowledge that fact for the record?"

"Of course, I was not driving my car on that date. In fact, I have not driven for months now!"

"Did you ever loan your car to anyone else?" Reed asked.

"Well, of course, when my niece Alicia finds time to come home she uses it!" Inga's cheeks were flushed and she straightened in her chair.

"Do you remember if she drove it on the night there was this crash?" Reed asked.

"Well, how would I know, she comes and goes!" Inga clasped her hands in her lap and Reed saw a faraway look come into her eyes just then. He waited a few minutes, and then asked, "Are you remembering something Inga?"

"I do remember that night now, it was late and I was watching out my bedroom window for my boyfriend to come over. You see, we were going to sleep a few hours and then leave to go to Las Vegas to get married." She wiped at a tear on her cheek.

"I know Inga," And he reached for a tissue from a box that stood on a table nearby. "Go on," he urged her then.

"Well, once when I looked I saw my car was gone and then later I saw it was there. So that must have been when she used it."

"She was home later in the evening then?" Reed asked.

"I remember now she was and she wasn't being very nice." Inga twisted her hands in her lap.

"What did she do?" Reed asked still taping the interview.

"Oh-, I don't like to have to do this," Inga said looking sad and shed another tear.

"Go on Inga, it'll be okay. Tell me why you are upset?" Reed felt sorry for the poor lady but if she was covering for her niece he had to find out.

Then Inga took a deep breath and said, "If my car was involved in an accident at that time, she was driving!"

Reed turned off the recording and put an arm over her shoulder and gave her a hug. "Inga, thank you and now what would you like to do? I can help you if you want to stay here or find another place where you would be happy. I'll come back in a day or so and help you with whatever you choose to do."

"Thank you, Reed, for helping me, I didn't know what to do." And she wiped another tear.

"Enjoy your new friends Inga and I'll be back soon," he said.

Next, he drove to the jail in downtown Billings and asked to see Jason Edwards.

He'd been arrested in the traffic chase the day before and held for growing cannabis with the attempt to sell and was being held awaiting a court date. Today the little creep was sitting in a corner of his cell away from several Native Americans who sat laughing. Jason had his arms clasped around his knees as if protecting himself from something they had apparently said. When he heard his name called he jumped up and ran to stand at the bars.

"Get me out of this hell-hole," he whined to Reed.

"Yeah?" Reed commented. "Edwards, you've got to give me something first!" He took the prisoner to a small room and the door was locked as they sat down.

"You got everything yesterday!" Edwards sneered.

"Nope we didn't. Your DNA came back today." Reed went on, "and this morning I got your records from the DMV and it seems you've been a busy man." He read some, "It says here you had been charged with three DUI's and you went missing when you should have appeared at the Montana Board of Admissions to register for a two year stay at a work house. You somehow got away so there was a warrant out for your arrest!" Then leaning down in his face,

Reed said, "And now we have a murder, what did you and that Alicia Mueller have planned?"

By now the young man had a green look on his face and jumped up saying, "Let me out, I'm going to be sick!" And he clamped a hand over his mouth. The door flew open then from the outside and he ran to the restroom and puked. Reed just followed and waited. He didn't feel sorry for him in this pathetic stage as he lay on the floor and moaned. And after a few minutes, Reed motioned for him to get up and follow him back to the same room.

"What did you have to do with the man found murdered in Inga Mueller's driveway? And why don't you fess up that you were driving drunk that night and hit Alicia Mueller who was driving her aunt's car?"

Edwards just laughed. "You're the big shot here, figure it out!"

Reed laughed too, and then slapped the table top hard making him jump. "Yep, I'm the big shot and I promise you I will see to it you get the fullest degree of prison time. Oh, those bulls in there will love seeing your fresh bod and will fight over you! They'll rip you a new one in no time!"

Edwards face got white as snow.

"Are you ready for that?" Reed asked breathing in his face.

"I am not going to jail," the man groaned.

"Well give me something and maybe I can talk to the authorities and make a deal that might make this easier for you. I can't promise, but I'll try." Reed stood up.

Edwards held his head in his hands, and his hair hung in sweaty tufts around his head. Seeing him now in the harsh light of the jail, he looked pretty pitiful. Then he stood up and kicked his chair across the small room. Reed jumped to his feet and had his .45 out and ready. As an inspector for the insurance company, Reed was licensed to carry.

"I'll use this if I have to, Edwards. Keep it up and you won't have to worry about your address. Did you kill that man?" Reed asked in a low deadly voice.

"I don't know what in the hell you're talking about!"

"Well, what do you know then Edwards?" Reed had lowered his gun.

"When I saw no one was in the car, I left the scene too because I didn't want to be identified. But I don't know anything about a fucking murder!"

"Well Edwards, you don't have to worry about an address yet for a few years." Reed said.

"Yeah? I want to talk to an attorney. I'm through talking to you!"

"Right," Reed agreed as by now he had all he needed to know.

-42-

Alicia Mueller had left Billings in a damn hurry to get away from all the commotion going on at her aunt's house. The sheriff had taken Inga in for questioning after finding the neighbor dead in her driveway and was holding her. They couldn't connect Alicia with this man's death as she had been miles away working with her group.

"But Alicia," Inga had whispered back then, "I don't remember going to the store that night!"

"Well, I was here and I remember hearing you start the car and go somewhere."

Inga twisted her hands and tied her bathrobe belt tighter. She stared at Alicia.

"Inga, I remember you mentioned you needed to get some milk and cereal for breakfast earlier that evening." Alicia commented.

But--, oh dear, then I must have!" Inga had muttered in her confusion.

The next few days Alicia dreamed that soon she would be adding a huge amount of cash to her stash and she would go to one of those islands she had read about. She could almost feel the cool water and the warm sands. She imagined wearing a bikini, dancing on the wharves and becoming a tanned, mysterious island woman. And, she kept herself busy so she didn't have time to dwell on shooting Inga's boyfriend. The old womanizer, who had been wooing Inga with attention and then plans for them to run off to Las Vegas and get married. She had never even used her gun for real before and thank God she had tossed it in a lake. He was not going to get his hands on her money. Of course, her aunt was totally naïve about life and loved all the sweet talk he had been whispering in her ear. Alicia remembered mentioning to her aunt that the man driving the pickup that hit her carried good insurance and would have to pay big money to get her car fixed. And Inga had undoubtedly whispered to her boyfriend she was coming in to a lot of money.

Alicia was the woman's only living relative and had no thoughts of taking care of her old aunt. No sir, she was going to get the hell away from the U.S. as soon as the check came in the mail, giving no thought to the fact that a court date was eminent first!

-43-

Lindy was sitting out in the lanai having her morning coffee, watching the surfers riding the waves out on the ocean. It was autumn in the Midwest but here in Hilton Head, by the great Atlantic, the foliage was still green and full. There were great tall pine trees, then of course the water oaks, which were home to the ever-growing gray moss that clung to its branches. It looked charming to tourists, but was actually a haven for insects, small rodents and snakes. That's why Lindy loved living by the ocean where she only had sand and sea around her. A shiver ran over her body when she was reminded of when she had first come to the islands and had seen her first alligator. She had rented a villa in a gated area with lovely ponds, walking paths, trees and bushes. And she was happily walking along concentrating on her stride on one of those first days when suddenly just a few yards ahead she saw them, sunning themselves on the banks of a pond. She had stood stock still, her heart in her throat. Then too late, remembered seeing signs that reminded everyone to "watch for alligators". Horrified at their enormous sizes and gross features, she spun on her heels and hardly remembered her trek back to her villa. That was why from then on, she only stayed at places right by the ocean as they weren't usually known to cross sandy beaches.

Lindy refilled her coffee cup and went back out to the lanai and sat. Today she was reminded of Reed and wondered where he was. By now he should have been out of her thoughts for good, but as always about this time she would begin to wonder. He had always been there for her when she had a problem and he had always figured out what to do for her, but did that mean they had a special bond or something? Lordy, she didn't know. She pictured some of their good times together but then remembered the times she had gotten restless. Damn, she had to remember, she just wasn't a small-town type of girl, and in the end always had to get the hell away!

Alright she said to herself sternly, enough of this trite thinking. And she went in to shower and get ready for her morning people who might need her today.

A short time later she was pleasantly surprised when her doorbell rang and she opened it to find her long lost artist friend Margaret Ames from across the border. The woman she had gotten to know while visiting her friend Monica in Monterrey, Mexico a few years ago.

"Oh my God, I don't believe this," Lindy said and gasped as the woman hugged her fiercely to her ample bosom.

"I had to find you, my dear." Margaret whispered, somewhat nervously.

After becoming friends in Mexico, they were having lunch together one day when Lindy had suddenly stood up and grabbed her new friend away from their table just seconds before a huge chandelier had fallen down and totally smashed it to bits as an earthquake swept through the town. Having been brought up in the Latin culture Margaret believed that Lindy had been gifted with a supernatural clairvoyance and had helped her get started in her business by spreading the word to her many friends and acquaintances that her friend had the "gift". It had turned into a full-fledged venture, and since she didn't charge for the meetings it was considered a hobby. But she welcomed tips! And of course, cash only.

"Come in my friend, it's so good to see you again," Lindy exclaimed excited, taking her arm and leading her into her house.

"I'm so glad, but I had a hard time finding you Lindy. I called your friend Monica and she finally gave me your address here in Hilton Head. I apologize I didn't have a cell phone number for you or I would have called ahead," Margaret said as she brushed a hand over her snow-white hair.

"That's okay Margaret, you're welcome in my home any time. I just haven't talked to Monica for a while." They went into the kitchen and Lindy pointed to a stool at her counter. "Sit and relax my friend and I'll make some coffee."

"That sounds heavenly, I haven't had a real cup of it since I left Mexico." Margaret took a deep breath and sat. As always, she looked like a million bucks as she was clad in a black pantsuit with a black belt and discreet diamonds in her ears. As a woman somewhere in her seventies, she was still slim and shapely in her high heels.

"I didn't know you had such a lovely home right here on the beach Lindy," Margaret said looking around.

"I've lived here for a while, do you like it?" Lindy asked as she set out cups and saucers.

"My dear it is lovely. And the ocean right out your door is dazzling!" Margaret's blue eyes lit up.

"Let's have our coffee out in the lanai while you tell me what's going," Lindy said and led the way out into the sun lit room carrying a tray. After sitting down and sipping their coffee, Margaret Ames began.

"Lindy, I have to tell you, I am so upset." She took a breath. "You see I've been losing things around my home!" The usually calm poised artist got tears in her eyes as she spoke.

"What do you mean Margaret? What kind of things?" Lindy asked.

"Like jewelry and then some small paintings I'd just finished." She took a breath and went on, "Lindy, I'm worried that I might be getting the dreaded Alzheimer's, or that I have thieves in my house."

"How long has it been since you started to realize things were missing?" Lindy saw that her friend looked sad and tired.

"Oh, I guess maybe around six months or so. At first, I thought I had just misplaced some of the jewelry pieces, but then it happened again. This time it was a small pair of diamond earrings, a pin and then a necklace of genuine black pearls that was a gift from my deceased husband." She wiped a sudden tear.

"Did you report this to the police?" Lindy wanted to know.

"A detective from the police department came over to see me, and by then I had missed several paintings that I was planning on sending out for a gallery show."

"What did he do?" Lindy asked.

"Really there was nothing he could do." Margaret emptied her coffee cup and Lindy refilled both of their cups. "He suggested I start to keep a better eye on my things." Margaret added.

Lindy had been to Margaret's home in Monterrey where she had a palatial house amongst beautiful grounds inside a gated area.

"How many people have access to your home?" Lindy asked curiously.

Margaret ran a hand over a cheek. "Too many but I seem to need them all."

"Tell me about them. What are their duties?"

And Margaret went on. "First of all, I have my housekeeper, she's a friend and has been with me for ten years and is in charge of keeping everyone on their toes."

"Does she hire the help for you?" Lindy asked.

"Yes, most of the time and I trust her implicitly," Margaret said, but with a worried look on her face.

"Do you have any new help?" Lindy asked then.

"Well no, but there's always strangers who come along, you know with the lawn service or the pool people. I had some remodeling done some months ago and then there were strangers in and out.

Just then Margaret's cell phone rang, and after a minute her face turned white and she whispered, "No! I'll be back as soon as possible!" She clicked off and turned to Lindy, then put her face in her hands.

"What is wrong Margaret?" Lindy asked.

"That was my neighbor, I can't believe this," she whispered and began to cry. "He said my housekeeper is dead! And they say she was murdered!"

"What?" Lindy jumped up from the couch and went to her side.

"Murdered, who would hurt such a good woman, a devout Catholic with a big family."

Lindy remembered meeting the housekeeper when she had been in Mexico and had been a guest at Margaret's home. Bella was her name and she was a native of Mexico.

"Come on, I have some good brandy and I'll make some tea," and Lindy took her arm and they went into the kitchen. Margaret sat on one of the stools at the counter and sipped the brandy while Lindy busied herself heating water and getting cups and saucers ready.

"I need to make some calls now while you do that," Margaret murmured regaining some composure. And when the tea was ready, Lindy set hers down and said, "I'm going to take a shower and give you some time for your calls.

Margaret nodded and began to dial.

Lindy stood in the shower as some real scary thoughts began to take shape in her head. She glimpsed three men racing through Margaret's house, guns in hand. She saw Bella hurt and bleeding crawling to get help. A girl stood watching and hurrying the men along, then left with them after more gun shots echoed. Lindy hurriedly finished and grabbed a towel, slipped on a robe, then rushed out to her friend.

"Bella died on the way to the hospital," Margaret said tearfully as she paced around the living room. "I just talked to my neighbor again and he said she was shot in the chest." She wiped tears off her cheeks.

"Do you have someone who can take care of things for you right now?" Lindy asked.

"Yes, I talked to my friend and attorney, Jamie Wolf, she is covering for me. Now I need to make arrangements to get back home right away."

"Margaret, why don't you charter a plane and then you can be there in a few hours?" Lindy suggested.

"Yes, yes I will. I'm just not thinking straight right now."

"I've got the number right here, I've never used this service but I'm sure they can steer you to the right place." Lindy offered opening her cell contact list to the number.

Margaret's visit was cut short and she was only able to spend the one day in Hilton Head with Lindy. She was now scheduled to fly back to Monterrey at nine o'clock that evening. But there was enough time for Lindy to tell her friend what she had seen in her visions.

"Margaret," Lindy said, "you have someone on your staff that cannot be trusted. When I was in the shower I saw a woman, maybe a girlfriend or a relative of someone in your employ, in your house seemingly knowing her way around, directing three men with gun!"

"You did? What did she look like?" Margaret asked jerking up straighter on her stool.

Lindy thought for a minute, "I'd say she is in her twenties, has long black hair and dark eyes, and a native of Mexico."

"Oh my God, I know who that is. That's Bella's granddaughter! She works at the house from time to time."

Evening was fast approaching on the island in South Carolina and the sun was sliding down in the west. Lindy made a crab salad and baked a loaf of bread earlier as they were sitting in the kitchen. Now she opened a bottle of wine and poured a glass of Pinot Grigio' for each of them.

"I bet you've not eaten anything today Margaret and it's going to be a long night for you. Try to eat something now." And she honestly tried, but she was too shaken by the death of Bella, her friend and housekeeper.

"I'm sorry Lindy, I just can't eat but I will have the wine." She apologized.

It was nearing the time for Margaret's hurried flight back to Monterrey and Lindy helped her into her Mercedes and they sped out to the airport in Hilton Head. As they waited for her to board her flight, Margaret enveloped Lindy in her arms and whispered, "Thank you Lindy for helping me see who is responsible for all this!" And then Margaret Ames was gone.

-44-

CeCe Jones danced and stripped down to the last G-string for the night and she was dog-tired. It had been long days of entertaining a convention of deer hunters, which came up once a year with her group being the head-liner with top billing. The money was terrific as the customers were pretty-loose with their cash.

Alicia had been tucking her money away for months, and with what she was going to get soon from Edwards's insurance company she was going to be so rich. When she was dancing for all the drunken hunters out there who were gawking at her body, she just pretended she was a beautiful Parisian ballerina performing for an adoring audience.

Finally finishing up their night, Clark their limo driver, stuck his head in the doorway to their dressing room and said, "Ten minutes ladies and we're out of here. You can count your money on the road and catch a nap as we've got a long ride ahead. When we get there, we'll have a day and a half to rest up and then we start at a place called "Daddy's Girls". Clark finished his business with the bar owner and minutes later had the limo pulled up to the back door of the building with the motor running.

Suddenly two men in suits tapped on his car window. And seeing they looked all business in suits and ties, Clark turned the window down. "Can I help you?" he asked.

They held up their credentials saying "We've got an all-points bulletin for a female named Alicia Mueller."

"Am I supposed to know her?" Clark asked.

"We've been informed that she's traveling with this group of entertainers!" The taller of the two commented.

"Sorry, I don't know anyone by that name. Excuse me now we have a deadline to meet." And Clark turned the window up as the four women suddenly clamored into the vehicle and the men had to jump back out of the way as the limo sped out of the parking lot and onto the freeway.

"Well, that went well, now what?" The short man said to the tall one.

"We'll call it in and leave a message. I've got my vacation starting in the morning tomorrow and if I don't get back to load up the wife and kids she'll be so pissed I won't get laid for a month!"

"Well, be damned if I'm going to chase after that woman by myself. I'll just tell the boss it was a bum steer."

"Good luck with it all. I for one am going to lie on a beach and let the world go by. See you in two weeks!"

-45-

Reed Conners left Jason Edwards jail cell and went in search of Sheriff Harding and was told the man was heading to his office after being in court. Reed took a seat in his inner office and began to check his notes for everything he needed to present to him. That Edwards was at fault? The man wouldn't admit that he didn't have a clear view of the road ahead when he was going through the intersection and now there was a murder in the mix.

Did this murder have anything to do with the insurance claim? Reed needed to talk to the sheriff about it again and see if he thought it had a connection.

After another ten minutes Harding came hurrying into his office and Reed stood up to greet him. "Good you're here Conners, I've had my men out canvasing Inga Mueller's neighborhood and we've got some new information." He shut the door into his office and they both sat down.

He went on to say, "A neighbor came forward after being on vacation and told us that on the morning of the shooting he was unloading his car and carrying in his suitcases, and as he was coming around the corner of his house he saw a light-colored car hesitate in front of Mueller's and then take off. It didn't belong to anyone from around the area."

"Okay, that's a start. Now the niece doesn't own a car and we know Inga's car was out of commission. Who was driving that vehicle as the timing for the murder is good. The man was shot at about that time!" Reed remarked.

"I've got my man over there now working with the neighbor for a better description of the car and as much of the driver as he can remember. He should be back here shortly," Sheriff Harding replied.

"Okay, so far I've got Edwards admitting he drove one car and Inga admitting she wasn't the driver of her Buick, so that leaves the niece as the driver. But Alicia Mueller claims she wasn't here at the time, that she was out of town working."

Sheriff Harding said, "Yeah? I've got an APB out for her, I want her brought in for questioning.

Reed stood up and said "I'll get back to you."

"Swell. I'll be in my office for the rest of the day. If not, my deputies will know where I am."

Reed left the sheriff's office and found a coffee shop. He needed another cup of some strong brew and not what most places called coffee, which to him tasted like a warm Norwegian tea. He found a small shop with booths that had a good aroma of fresh coffee as he came in the door. He laid out his notes and patiently went over all he had so far as he drank the strong brew. He knew in his gut Alicia Mueller was involved up to her neck in this. That her Aunt Inga was too bewildered to have thought out this insurance claim. But did Alicia kill that neighbor? Yes, he said to himself, she did! But now I need that neighbor's information and fast! And I don't want Edwards to wrangle his way out of jail on that charge of growing weed for sale, as he's involved in this as well! As soon as that deputy gets back with the neighbor's drawing of the car they should be able to track that down and fast.

Reed decided to have a sandwich for lunch as it was going into the afternoon, and he was just finishing a cup of fresh tomato soup when his cell vibrated on the table.

"Connors," Reed answered.

"Harding here, come on back, I've got a good picture." Reed hurriedly paid up and went back to the sheriff's office.

"Here, take a look. I don't recognize the vehicle, but it is a late model." Sheriff Harding exclaimed.

Reed took his time. "Okay, we know it was a light color, maybe beige. We know it slowed down and hesitated in front of the Mueller's house that morning."

"I've been thinking, could the niece have rented a car and driven here and shot the guy?" Harding asked.

"We think alike," Reed said.

"Yes, the APB I sent out for this Alicia Mueller covers Montana, Minnesota, North and South Dakota so we should hear something soon now," the sheriff commented and blew out a tired breath. "I've got other cases that need my attention so Christ, I'm really bogged down right now!"

"Understandably so." Reed remarked. "I'll stick close so please give me a call when you hear something.

A few hours later Reed got a call from Sheriff Harding saying that as yet, nothing had turned up.

-46-

Lindy drove back home after taking Margaret Ames to the airport for her hurried return trip back to Monterrey Mexico. Lordy, she had been so distraught when she first arrived to see Lindy about a problem going on in her home. As they had sat later in the living room, Lindy told Margaret of the vision she had of the robbery that had taken place in Margaret's home that day. Margaret's dear friend and housekeeper Bella had been shot and later died. Of seeing Bella's granddaughter leading the robbing thieves through her house and leaving with them with bags filled with her things. Lindy didn't hesitate at telling Margaret every detail. The poor woman had look terrified hearing what was going on right there in her home. But after a few minutes she wiped her eyes and took a calming breath and said, "And to think this young girl apparently had ulterior motives when she'd come and worked with her grandmother at the house. Poor Bella would be just sickened to know her family had done something like this!"

Margaret had gotten on the chartered plane still feeling terribly upset. She had come to see Lindy because she needed answers; when at first, she had thought she had just misplaced things and they would eventually show up, but they never had. She had feared that someone in her home was stealing, and it broke her heart as she took great care of her staff, at things like birthdays and holidays. And now to know that Bella was dead and her granddaughter was behind the scandalous theft going on in her house.

Lindy had thought of insisting she go along with Margaret home to Monterrey, Mexico but hadn't dare pursue the idea as she remembered she would be too close to the D'Agustino families compound as Margaret lived in the same affluent area. She just couldn't take the chance of running into any of them. For just a minute though, Lindy remembered that warm feeling she'd had so long ago of being so in love with Mario. Oh, how she had glowed with it and then how he had doused the flame by murdering that man while they had been out on the ocean. She felt lucky that she hadn't gotten killed too when the FBI stepped into the picture and she had to testify against him in court. A long time ago, she sighed pensively.

She drove through the streets of Hilton Head where the plants and flowering bushes were ablaze with their colors. The kale was dark green with a white lacy border and a huge pink center. Variations of this plant were abundant around the island, as it thrived in the hot moist climate. Back home now, she took a fresh cup of coffee out to the lanai and sat back and relaxed. When she had first bought her home, she'd had the front and sides of her yard landscaped with the native grass of the south, pink azalea and purple lilac bushes. Bamboo trees were planted around the perimeter. And of course, here too, kale was showcased in its own flowering beds. An irrigation system was set to come on early each morning to water and freshen the whole area. In the back by the water's edge, she found a huge old log aged to silver, and set it out so anyone walking by who needed to take a rest could sit for a while and gaze out at the waters ever changing scene.

Early the next morning, before anyone needing her visionary guidance arrived, Lindy had time to just sit and relax. She had slid the glass doors to the side on the lanai so she had a full view of the ocean. The salt air tickled her nose and the humidity flattened her blonde tresses, but it was wonderful. However, sometimes she felt lonely and wished she had someone to share this loveliness with. Reed came to mind first, but he was a hunter who loved the lakes and wilderness of the north. He'd been down several times, and liked the water and the lifestyle, but only as a visitor. Over time she had invited a few acquaintances to share her home but never had found anyone who she'd want to wake up with every day.

Lordy, oh well, she thought standing up and taking a last look at the water before going in to take a shower and get ready for her people. It's just me! And she put a smile on her face and found her happy place as she walked through her beautiful home.

A short time later, showered and dressed for the day, Lindy peeked out and then opened her door for her first customer and the first thing she saw was the barrel of a gun pointed right at her face!

-47-

Reed had left his hotel early and went to see if Inga was still in that home she had been sent to. He found her again sitting amongst a group of people talking and laughing at a large round table apparently eating breakfast. The appetizing aroma of coffee and bacon was heavy in the air as he came into the dining room. Inga jumped up and smiled, amidst teasing whispers from her new friends.

"Mr. Connors how lovely to see you again, but have you come to take me back to my house?" The smile on her face faded as she asked. Today she was dressed in a pink jogging outfit with matching lipstick, and when she waved her hands in greeting her matching pink nail polish glowed.

"No Inga, remember I said I would be back. Why don't you go and finish your breakfast and I'll stick around until you're done?"

"Really? Thanks, I'll just be a few minutes." She hurried back to her table and a few minutes later she returned and they sat down.

"What's going on?" She asked.

"Inga, have you heard from your niece?" Reed asked.

"No, but what makes you think I would have?" Inga commented. "I hardly ever do."

"Well, I'm just checking. Do you know where to find her?"

"Well, no not right off, but she works in some office here downtown.

"So, she says she has a job here in Billings? Does she have an apartment here in town?" Reed asked curiously.

"Oh goodness, I can't keep up with her. She doesn't come home often and she stays with friends a lot too!" Inga started to wring her hands and tears came into her eyes.

"Inga, I don't mean to upset you. Do you like it here?" Reed asked.

"Oh yes, you see now that my boyfriend died I'm so lonely. Do you think I can live here now?" Inga asked hopefully.

"I should think so. I will find out how to make the arrangements. You just relax and enjoy your new friends."

Before Reed left the home, he talked to the Administer and a facilitator who assured him they would take good care of Inga and help her with the decisions so she could live there permanently.

He had gotten a message last night that the sheriff's department had learned that Alicia was traveling with the group of strippers in the Dakotas, but that covered two whole states and hundreds of miles. How the hell could he find and catch up with them? Then he remembered seeing them when he'd first gotten to Billings and stopped in for a quick drink at that rat hole bar. That was when he'd noticed the big birthmark one dancer had on her neck that spread up to the side of her face. She'd covered it with her hair but when she took a bow her hair had swished aside. He'd seen it again when Alicia Mueller opened the door at Inga Mueller's house when he'd first come to town.

He got in the Corvette then and circled around the blocks and finally found the bar where the troop of dancers had been booked. He found out they were called "Clark's Review" and then traced them to the spot they would be appearing the next night, a joint called "Daddy's Girls" in North Dakota. He went back to Sheriff Harding's office.

"Here's what I found out, Alicia Mueller is in Fargo, North Dakota. What do you think of the idea about talking to the police up there and asking if one of their men could accompany me to the club and we take her in for questioning?"

Harding thought for a minute. "That woman is guilty of murder and I want to close this damn case. Christ, I've got a laundry list of violations she has committed! Here's what we'll do. I'll issue a warrant to bring her in for questioning and call the department in Fargo and ask for their help. Now when you pick her up, I want her immediately transported back here to face her charges." The sheriff got busy on the phone making the necessary arrangements as Reed left and got on the road. It was late morning and he figured by the time he got there the dancers would be well into their entertainment showing off their stuff. Checking into the police department in Fargo, Reed hooked up with a detective.

"Names Dick Anderson," the man said reaching out his hand. "I got the low down from the boss. So, I understand we get to check out a "tittie show!" Anderson exclaimed with a twinkle in his eye. He was near retirement age with blondish gray hair, a trimmed beard and slim body.

"Yeah, that's the plan!"

Anderson went on to say, "We're going to bring the woman back here and we'll hold her in our precinct until Billings will take over."

So, amidst crashing music and a booming drum beat, the two men walked into the club and found seats near the back. This was the second time Reed had seen the show and was again amazed at the amount of money that landed on the stage floor. And so as not to stand out they clapped and cheered as the women took their turns doing the bump and grind. A couple of times they were actually embarrassed and winked at each other.

"Damn, how did she do that?" Anderson mumbled watching CeCe's antics as she whirled around the pole.

And then it was all over and all four women came on stage and took their bow and more bills flew through the air. Reed and Anderson got up quickly and went backstage and as CeCe, Alicia Mueller, flew into the room the two men flanked her.

"Alicia Mueller, we have a warrant to pick you up and bring you in for questioning," Reed said and spun her around and cuffed her.

"What the fuck--," Alicia yelled and turned to run. But both Dick Anderson and Reed stood in her way and Reed went on. "We're taking you into custody to the Fargo precinct here and then you'll be transported back to Billings, Montana to face charges!"

"Charges, what the hell for?" Alicia asked sarcastically.

Reed took the arrest warrant out of his pocket. "It says here, 'For questioning in a murder and insurance fraud!"

Her face paled and then turned beet red as she yelled, "Screw you!"

-48-

Lindy sucked in her breath as she had opened the front door and looked right into the end of the gun barrel that was pointed at her head. She jerked back and slammed the door just seconds away from getting blasted in the face. She flipped the locks on and ran to the side door and did the same. She had the hardware that an ambitious salesman at a trade show had talked her into spending big bucks on and this was the first time she had a reason to use it. "A fine lady like you living alone should have this on her home for safety," He proclaimed. And she had bought the steel lined doors and locks and had them installed along with a security system. Now she stood still and listened. If a window should be raised or broken an alarm would go off. Right now, she could hear soft footsteps creeping around the house to the back, which looked out on the beach. Here too the glass doors on the lanai were all wired and so there was no way to get in short of breaking the glass.

"Asshole!" Lindy yelled loudly and her right hand closed over the gun in her pocket as she dialed 911. When the call was answered she whispered, "There's someone trying to get in my house and he has a gun! I live at 2000 Beach Drive."

"Are all your doors and windows locked?" she was asked.

"Yes, hurry!" Lindy whispered.

She had lived alone a lot over the years and there had been a few times when she had been really afraid, mainly at night but this was the middle of the day. And she'd found then to give herself the bravery to get out of bed and investigate instead of lying there scared stiff, she had to do something and that's when she found if she yelled and screamed she got herself pissed and would get some nerve. Now she began to do just that as she walked through her rooms with her gun pointed and ready. Ten minutes later, as she peeked out a window she saw a police cruiser slowly circling around her block. Finally, after several hours and a snifter of brandy, Lindy calmed down after getting a call that the police would be in the area checking throughout the next twenty-four hours. To get her mind off the episode she decided to get out of the house and at Shirlee's Place found her friend sitting at her piano running over some new numbers she was learning for the evening show.

"Nice to see you," Shirlee commented as she got up and came over to the bar.

"Girlfriend, it's been awhile" Lindy said as she sipped a tall mimosa. "I've been meaning to stop in but time flies and I think I'm busy!"

"Well, aren't you? I heard from a friend that you're flooded with folks needing your aid!"

"Well, yes I was until today." Lindy murmured.

"Why, did something happen?" Shirlee asked.

Lindy wrinkled her forehead. "Yes unfortunately. I opened my door for my first client and found a gun pointed at me!"

"Really! What was that about?" Shirlee sat down on the next stool at the bar and went on, "What did you do?"

Lindy shook her head, "I slammed the door or within seconds I would have gotten my head blown off."

"Good Lord, who do you suppose it was?" Shirlee asked.

"I just had a fleeting glance and it was a man. But of course, by the time the police got there he had disappeared. It was just hours ago!" Lindy grimaced. "That's why I had to get out of there!"

"Well, stay here for now. But tonight, come home with me and stay for a day or two."

"Thanks, my friend," Lindy said and leaned over, "But I'm a big girl and I have a big shooter."

"Well okay, think about it," Shirlee said. "But what are you going to do?"

"I'm thinking of getting a dog, a killer dog," Lindy exclaimed.

"But do you like dogs?" Shirlee wanted to know.

"No, no I don't like animals in the house!" Lindy said and almost laughed if it wasn't so serious.

"Well hell," Shirlee looked at her friend and shook her head. "Here's an idea, you should hire a big guy to guard you. I know a few who would scare the bejesus out of anyone snooping around your place."

Lindy looked at her friend and paused. "Let me think about that." And she drank some more of her mimosa and commented, "Okay, where would you find these big strong guys?"

"Well, first of all I know a guy by the name of Troy, who hires out to guard stars who come to the island. And then another who is a detective, now he would scare the hell out of anyone creeping around your place."

It didn't take Lindy long to make a decision. "Okay I need someone like that to catch this asshole. Could you get in touch with them to see if it would be something either of them would do?"

Shirlee stood up. "I'll go to my office and make some calls right now."

Lindy sat at the bar and nursed her drink and within thirty minutes Shirlee was back saying, "Troy is on a job right now for a few days, but Detective Joe Brown is on his way here now. See what you think!" And Lindy ordered another mimosa and waited curiously for this person.

No more than thirty minutes went by and a man at least six feet four strolled up to the bar and looked around for Shirlee. As she stood up he took her in to his arms and swung her into a dip and a kiss.

"My beautiful songstress," he murmured standing her up and laughing.

"Joe," Shirlee said smiling, "this is my friend Lindy Lewis whom I'd like you to meet. Lindy this is Detective Joe Brown."

And Lindy stood up and reached a hand over. He took hers and kissed it.

Shirlee leaned over and said, "Don't let his charm fool you Lindy, I promise you he can be a real bad ass!"

"So, this is the beautiful lady who needs help?" And he pulled another bar stool over.

Lindy gazed at the man. He was tanned with a firm jaw, and muscles on his arms and chest bulged under his tennis whites. His eyes were dark and his black hair was tied in a ponytail. His manner was relaxed.

Shirlee stood up saying, "I'll send over a beer for you Joe and I'll leave you two to talk."

Joe Brown slid over closer and grinned. "Okay, tell me what you need young lady."

And Lindy went into detail and after agreeing on a price and a time to start, they shook hands and both departed agreeing to meet at her house in an hour. He said he would not be leaving his vehicle around her place at any time and he smiled saying, "Relax, you will not even know I'm there."

When he came over later that day, Lindy showed him a guest bedroom and bath he could use. That night she went to bed relieved knowing there was a man in the house with a bigger gun then she had. And the next day her people were waiting as usual for her only now a new pair of eyes was ever watchful.

It was a peaceful morning with only three people needing her candid offering of counsel, without any interference from another attack. The afternoon and evening wore on quietly as Joe Brown did his walk around inside checking doors and windows staying out of view and after dark took up a vantage post outside. Lindy had made him some dinner and put it in the refrigerator to eat whenever he wanted with the invitation to help himself to water and soda. The second night Lindy sat out in the lanai with a glass of wine and watched the lights from the large ships and smaller crafts sailing across the ocean. It had been arranged between Joe and her to see if this would draw the person out, and he would be close to pounce on the offender. But nothing happened after a few hours so Lindy closed and locked the lanai doors and closed the drapes.

She went to bed the third night wondering if she should just let Joe go, as it must have been just a onetime thing and the guy with the gun must have moved on. She closed her eyes really liking the safe cocoon she was in.

It was late in the night when she heard the soft rustle of the window blind being raised. Her eyelids flew open and she lay frozen as she heard it slide up slowly. Something caught her eye at the side of her bed just inches from her and then a hand clamped over her lips just in time to stifle her scream. Her thoughts whirled in confusion. The intruder was right by her bedside! And right then Lindy fainted dead away.

She came to as she heard grunts and cussing then saw a pile of moving bodies rolling around on the carpeted floor in the moonlight. Then she recognized Joe Brown as he cuffed a man and at gun point marched him out of her room. Lindy jumped up and found her robe and followed them out.

"Who the hell are you?" She yelled at the stranger. He wasn't anyone she recognized.

"We'll soon find out," Joe Brown growled and pushed him outside on the patio. Just then the police drove up and two officers jumped out and came up.

"He had a knife," the detective said and it's still in her bedroom on the floor.

"Well, well Greenwood," one said looking at the prisoner as he came closer. "I see you got your ass caught, you'll be looking at least twenty!" And they led the cuffed man over and locked him in the back of their squad car.

"A drifter after lone women", they told Detective Joe Brown.

Lindy fell into a chair and since she was too stressed to go back to bed, she sipped a brandy or two. And later that night, she dreamed of being safely in Reed's arms in his bed in Birch Lake.

-49-

Reed drove back to Billings from Fargo, North Dakota and checked back into the Northern Hotel. He had been gone for several nights and now he slept soundly. It was the weekend and Alicia Mueller was safely tucked in a cell, right next to Jason Edwards so they were probably keeping each other company.

Reed's dreams were the usual rehashing of his case and its possible outcome. He had the main contenders tied up in jail and it was now up to the court to figure out what to do with them. He finally tossed a too hard pillow on the floor and closed his eyes again.

The bed felt firm and the covers silken. In his dream tonight, he could smell Lindy's familiar perfume, the flowery scent of her hair and then the soft feel of her body as he held her close. He felt himself take a deep relaxing breath and fall deeper into a contented sleep. It seemed so right.

The next day was Sunday and he spent the day reading in the papers about the case and catching up on the news from the Midwest. It was harvest time around his hometown for wheat and soybeans, and although he had never been involved in farming he was familiar with it. He thought about the golden days of autumn, and he just had to get on the road home soon!

Monday morning dawned cool and sunny in the western state. Reed slipped on his boots and leather jacket and sped downtown in Billings. The streets were just coming alive with the morning commuters and residents hurrying to their places of employment. Even a horse or two could be seen cantering down the bricked and paved streets. Reed was not quite sure who had the right of way, but he tended to lean toward the horse.

He stopped in Sheriff Harding's office and found a chair to wait until the man got off the phone and then asked, "Has anything come down from upstairs yet?" Meaning had the District Attorney made any decisions yet on what to charge Alicia Mueller and Jason Edwards with.

Sheriff Harding ran a hand through his bushy mustache. "The place is slow on Mondays but it should be soon now."

"Well," Reed blow out a breath, "they better not just throw a fine at those two sitting up there and let them out. My boss will be pissed if he loses five million!"

Harding shook his head, "Edwards should get a tough one in the big house for growing weed for market and then for his involvement in the accident." He slid some files to the floor and sat back and put his feet on the desk.

"Jesus, I'm glad we got that Mueller woman in lock up, as yet we only have one witness who saw that she was driving that car that morning, the same time the man was found shot. Maybe after being locked up for a while, she's ready to talk."

"Yeah, sometimes they will cry like a baby!"

"I'd like to see these two this morning. Think you could hold off things for thirty minutes if the DA calls?" Reed asked. And he hurried over to the next building where the jail was. The minute he stepped in the door he got the sickening whiff of cigarettes, urine, sweat and fear.

He stopped at Alicia Mueller's cell. The woman was sitting in there with a blanket over her shoulders and when Reed came over to her cell she looked up.

"How are you today Miss Mueller," he asked. "Has your attorney shown up yet?"

She stood up, "I decided I don't need one. What the hell have you got anyway?" Today her face was devoid of make-up and her blond hair was straight and limp. The birthmark on the side of her face and neck stood out in the harsh light and he remembered the first time he had seen it in that bar.

Goddamn, Reed thought, the arrogance of this woman. No wonder she had her Aunt Inga snowed into believing she was the driver of the car in that accident.

"Are you prepared to meet the judge in court today then?" Reed asked.

"Why not?" Alicia said defensively, "There's no evidence to tie me to anything you've found!"

"Yeah, even if I tell you someone saw you when you shot that neighbor?" Reed remarked.

Alicia jumped up and the blanket fell to the floor. "I don't believe you!" She yelled. "I wasn't there and I've got people who will vouch for me!"

"Don't count on it," Reed said and turned to go. "You're facing twenty-five to life for murder!"

"Wait a goddamn minute," Alicia yelled again. "I wasn't even here in town!"

"Tell it to the judge Miss Mueller. He's got enough to hang you." And Reed walked out satisfied he had stirred her up."

At promptly nine o'clock, Sheriff Harding and Reed Conners were summoned to one of the rooms in the courthouse. Jason Edwards had been booked, fingerprinted and photographed the day before and now waited to be charged.

"Mr. Edwards, here's what you're accused of; taking some other person's property to live on, by the way it's called squatting, I charge you with trespassing and fine you five thousand dollars. Now as to your farming on the property growing marijuana for sale, and by the way I had immediately sent a crew over there to plow it up, I'm sentencing you to ten years in prison."

Jason Edwards gulped and his face turned beet red, apparently again realizing the money he had been dreaming of was lost.

"Now on to the next charges, your blood alcohol level was over the top when you were driving and got involved in an accident, so you will be spending forty-eight months in the work house with the loss of your driver's license forever as you don't deserve the privilege!"

The judge looked ornery but went on, "Mr. Edwards, you will be bound over to the courts for a trial date and you will be held without bail. Bailiff, take this man out of my court now!" And Jason Edwards was escorted out of the room.

Next up was Alicia Mueller. She still wore her wrinkled clothes, no make-up only now she had twisted her hair into a knot on her head. She too had been fingerprinted, had her picture taken and was awaiting arraignment this morning.

"Young lady," the judge said, "I spent some time catching up with your agenda and you should be ashamed of yourself of the way you have treated your poor old aunt. She took you in and raised you, and now you have been trying to inject a sense of bewilderment in her thoughts. I know the story Miss and I'm relieved to hear someone stepped up and got Inga Mueller into a place where she's happy and being cared for. For falsely accusing Inga Mueller of being the driver of that Buick of hers when that accident occurred, when you were the driver, I fine you ten thousand dollars and take your license for life for driving under the influence and leaving the scene of the accident.

Alicia's face was white. "No- that old bat was driving the car," she yelled.

The judge rapped his gavel. "Quiet down Miss Mueller. Now we have you involved with a murder. How do you plead?" He asked, "Be careful how you answer that." He went on to say, 'If you plead not guilty we go to trial and let me make you aware there is a witness ready to confirm seeing you in a beige car and hearing a shot at the time that morning when a man was found dead in Inga Mueller's driveway. I hear that the deceased was dating Inga Mueller, and that you saw him as a threat to the insurance claim she had with Federated Insurance for five million dollars. You claimed she needed constant medical care for the duration of her life because of the accident caused by Jason Edwards."

Reed kept an eye on Alicia as the judge read the report out loud. He saw her face turn from anger to fear.

"How do you plead Miss Mueller?"

All eyes were on her and she stood up and began to cry and said haltingly, "I took good care of my dear aunt for years and listened to her constant whining. But I loved her and worried about her always." Alicia shed big tears looking like the victim.

"How do you plead?" the judge repeated. All eyes were on her again waiting for her answer.

"Not guilty!" She said then. "I am not going to prison," she yelled hysterically, "I'll kill myself first, I will!" She sank to the floor covering her face for a few minutes, then suddenly stood up and yelled with a righteous look on her face. "I shot that asshole who was sweet talking my Aunt Inga. Don't you see? I had no choice! He was just some sleaze who wanted to marry her after hearing she was going to get a big insurance check. I was looking out for her!"

"Bailiff, take this woman into custody," the judge exclaimed, "and I charge her with murder!" In minutes Alicia Mueller was in handcuffs again on her way to a long stay behind bars.

And it didn't take long for Reed to pack and turn the Corvette toward Birch Lake. He was going home!

-50-

Shirlee noticed the lines on Lindy's face and the bags under her eyes. "Maybe you're just still jumpy after what happened, but Joe Brown got the man who was stalking and following you all these months."

"I know, but for some reason I still feel so uneasy." Lindy blew out a breath.

"Are you sleeping okay?" Shirlee asked.

"That's another thing, I'm not! And I have times where I feel so overheated."

Shirlee commented, "Maybe my friend, you've started menopause!"

"What, you have to be old!" Lindy grimaced and was highly offended.

They were having lunch again in a little café out on a wharf in Harbor Town.

Shirlee smiled and put an arm around her shoulders. "Why don't you see your doctor and talk this over with him. They have some tests now that can help you decide how to deal with this".

Then she added, "If that's the problem!"

"Well, I've got to think about it," Lindy whispered and looked around to see if anyone from the surrounding tables might have overheard their conversation.

"I hope you not upset at me for mentioning this are you?"

"No, no not from you," Lindy answered. "But I've got to admit I certainly wasn't thinking that was the problem. But thinking back, I remember my mom would be wearing sleeveless shirts even in the winter when she was older."

"Oh my, that poor girl, but remember in those days they didn't have the treatments we have now."

"Well, I suppose I should follow through. However, I don't have a doctor here in Hilton Head."

"I can give you the name of my gynecologist who is in Savannah, so it's an hour drive over there. And I could come along and we could have dinner and take in a show."

"Well okay, but I'm still not old enough to have something like that, you'll see!"

However, a week later the two women walked out of the medical center in Savannah with Lindy clutching the sample of Premarin they had given her for hormone replacement for menopause.

She was still in denial as she did not think she was that old! Well maybe she was--, hell she didn't know if she wanted to cry or swear! But in the next week Lindy had to grudgingly admit she was sleeping sound again.

"So that must be what was wrong," she had to admit to Shirlee who had called to check on her friend.

"There you go. That wasn't so hard was it?" Shirlee commented.

"Well, at the time it was, but you can't fool Mother Nature, so it's okay." Lindy said drily.

She didn't say anything to her friend, but she had spent the last few days thinking of only that. It had come like a bolt of lightning when she realized all of a sudden, she was too old now to bear children! Not that she had planned on it, but always just knowing she had the option. Now that time had passed and she felt terribly saddened.

Shirlee went on and asked, "What are you going to do today?"

Lindy was quiet for a minute, and then just said it out loud, what she had made up her mind to do. "My friend," she said, "after much soul searching and after what I've learned about myself, I've decided to call

Reed. I need to talk to him about us." She sighed, "That's if there still is a chance! Just thinking about it scares the hell out of me, but I need to do it now, today and Lordy not waste another day!"

"I've always known you love the guy Lindy," Shirlee said, "So don't you dare throw away any more time!"

Later, after a couple of sips of brandy Lindy picked up her cell and made the call. And when Reed's voice echoed across the miles her heart reeled at the memory of how safe she felt hearing it again.

***

Reed had just cleaned up his boat before storing it for the winter when his cell phone began to vibrate in his shirt pocket. He had been having some moments of loneliness after getting back to his house in Birch Lake so when he saw it was Lindy calling his breath hitched. He walked over to a bench by a stand of pine trees and sat down.

"Lindy," He growled not sure how his heart would react this time. But he heard the tremor in her voice.

"Reed, it's me." She said hesitating and then plunging on, "First of all I need to apologize for leaving. I'm sorry!"

Reed took his time and then said, "Lindy, you say you're sorry but how do you think I feel? Why did you do it again?"

She swallowed tears, she was not going to cry as she went on, "I guess I just wasn't ready to get serious. And I thought I would stay young forever and I didn't want to miss out!"

"Miss out on what? How did you think I felt not knowing where you were?"

"Well, Reed how do you think I felt when you would take off for weeks at a time for your job, why didn't you ever ask me to go along?"

Reed didn't say anything for a minute. "I'm sorry about that Lindy I guess I just didn't realize you would get lonely."

"All those days and weeks wasted!" She grabbed a tissue and wiped a tear. And went on, "Reed I'm wondering," She whispered tentatively, "I love you and miss you--, could we try again?"

Maybe-, he hesitated. Then thought of that little black box with the large diamond he had bought and put in the back of the closet. Maybe there was a chance now after all!

He said then, "Lindy I'm leaving on the next flight to Hilton Head, South Carolina!"

And with the glow of hope, Lindy thought just maybe it wasn't too late for her and Reed after all.

The End

Not sure what to read next?

Catch up with these!

THE LINDY LEWIS ADVENTURES

MOONBEAMS

MOONBEAMS TOO

ALMIGHTY

ALMIGHTY TOO

**Order books on line at;
lynmillerbooks.com**

Or email me at lindylewis1@msn.com

Lyn Miller LaCoursiere

Lyn Miller LaCoursiere lives in Minneapolis and has published numerous newspaper articles dealing with life and its challenges. This is her eleventh novel which again takes place in the Midwest.

52860526R00209

Made in the USA
Lexington, KY
23 September 2019